A PLUME BOOK

THE BOOK OF JONAS

STEPHEN DAU is from western Pennsylvania and lives in Brussels. He worked for ten years in postwar reconstruction and international development prior to studying creative writing at Johns Hopkins University and Bennington, where he received an MFA. His work has appeared in *McSweeney's*, the *Pittsburgh Post-Gazette*, on MSNBC, and elsewhere. *The Book of Jonas* is his first novel.

Praise for *The Book of Jonas*

"A humane and unforgettable portrayal of the lives behind those casualty counts . . . Dau beautifully addresses a need to emotionally engage with a war that has been going on for ten years but that so often feels remote and unreal. . . . It is the first [novel of 2012] to feel genuinely important."

—*The Wall Street Journal*

"In moments, Dau's riffs on the young man's life recall the dense beauty of Michael Ondaatje's *The English Patient*. Like that book, [*The Book of Jonas*] is a tale obsessed with the way war can fracture memory and cauterize the place where love can begin. . . . If only our news had such radical belief in the power of empathy."

—*The Boston Globe*

"[S]pare prose . . . enhances the remarkably meager body of twenty-first-century wartime literature and identifies Pittsburgh as a site of divine intervention . . . the embodiment of truth and a symbol of human frailty; a record of war, a labor of love, and a tangible connection to lost ideals."

—Sandra Levis, *Pittsburgh Quarterly*

"Everything's a shock to the system for Jonas, a teenager from an unnamed Central Asian country, when he's granted asylum in the U.S. His struggles to assimilate and come to terms with his life—and the American soldier who saved it—make a story that could have been spun from yesterday's headlines. But in Stephen Dau's careful hands, it touches the deepest truths of loss and healing."

—Barnes & Noble

"Dau creates a disturbing portrayal of war as it destroys ideals and innocence and makes victims of civilians and soldiers alike. The novel is composed in a way that's similar to how a painter creates with watercolors: with delicate, barely substantive layers that blend together to reveal depth, nuance, and meaning. . . . Dau demonstrates the tragic paradoxes of war in this brilliant and deceptively simple novel that will provide ample discussion for high school classes studying Middle East conflicts."

—*School Library Journal*

THE
BOOK
OF
JONAS

STEPHEN DAU

A PLUME BOOK

PLUME
Published by the Penguin Group
Penguin Group (USA) Inc., 375 Hudson Street, New York, New York 10014, U.S.A. •
Penguin Group (Canada), 90 Eglinton Avenue East, Suite 700, Toronto, Ontario,
Canada M4P 2Y3 (a division of Pearson Penguin Canada Inc.) • Penguin Books
Ltd., 80 Strand, London WC2R 0RL, England • Penguin Ireland, 25 St. Stephen's
Green, Dublin 2, Ireland (a division of Penguin Books Ltd.) • Penguin Group
(Australia), 707 Collins Street, Melbourne, Victoria 3008, Australia (a division of
Pearson Australia Group Pty. Ltd.) • Penguin Books India Pvt. Ltd., 11 Community
Centre, Panchsheel Park, New Delhi – 110 017, India • Penguin Group (NZ),
67 Apollo Drive, Rosedale, Auckland 0632, New Zealand (a division of Pearson
New Zealand Ltd.) • Penguin Books (South Africa), Rosebank Office Park, 181 Jan
Smuts Avenue, Parktown North 2193, South Africa • Penguin China, B7 Jiaming
Center, 27 East Third Ring Road North, Chaoyang District, Beijing 100020, China

Penguin Books Ltd., Registered Offices: 80 Strand, London WC2R 0RL, England

Published by Plume, a member of Penguin Group (USA) Inc. Previously published
in a Blue Rider Press edition.

First Plume Printing, March 2013
1   3   5   7   9   10   8   6   4   2

The Library of Congress has catalogued the Blue Rider Press edition as follows:

Dau, Stephen.
The book of Jonas / Stephen Dau.
p. cm.
ISBN 978-0-399-15845-2 (hc.)
ISBN 978-0-452-29897-2 (pbk.)
I. Title.
PS3604.A87B66 2012
813'.6—dc23   2011047494

Printed in the United States of America
Original hardcover design by Michelle McMillian

PUBLISHER'S NOTE
This is a work of fiction. Names, characters, places, and incidents are either the
product of the author's imagination or are used fictitiously, and any resemblance to
actual persons, living or dead, business establishments, events, or locales is entirely
coincidental.

FOR
CLAUDIA
AND
SERAPHINA

THE
BOOK
OF
JONAS

PROCESSIONAL

They arrived like a thought, tracing contrails across the deep sky as though writing out their intentions in letters too big to be fully seen from the earth. Or they flowed low and fast over the hills, their great machines arcing silently from horizon to horizon, so fast that they were there and gone before the roar from their engines caught up, screaming the news of their arrival even as they disappeared.

In the village they tried to make sense of it.

The imam said that the Americans were like the lion who had stepped on a thorn, and then went about making a great noise, roaring at the world from his pain. But it would soon pass, he said, when the thorn dried up and fell out, when the pain ebbed, and then tranquillity would be restored.

Younis's father, on the other hand, said that no, this was only the beginning. The planes in the sky were like the first gray dusting of blight on the wheat, which this year might only affect a few sheaves, but which would spread over time, draining the golden crop of its color, rendering it foul and devoid of life.

Most of the villagers tended toward one or the other of these two points of view. But the discussions between them, while occasionally animated, as were most of their discussions, whether about God, or cricket, or livestock, lacked any real vehemence or certainty. The positions staked out were not hard and fixed, but were instead general inclinations to support one side or the other.

Because, in fact, nobody knew what to make of the visitors in the sky. No one could say for sure whether they were a temporary nuisance, as the imam thought, or a harbinger of disaster, as Younis's father said, or even, as a very few dared to profess, brought with them tidings of better days ahead.

So they carried on as usual, bending over their scythes in their fields, or walking the low pastures with their flocks and their dogs. And whenever they spotted a line of smoke, high and pale like the daytime moon, or heard the jets echo from the surrounding mountains, they would look up, and then turn to one another and talk about what it meant as though discussing something large and remote and uncontrollable, like the weather.

INVOCATION

I

What is it like to lose everything?

Younis was first asked this question by a well-meaning development worker, a friendly young man whose specialty was working in war zones. They sat across from each other in cheap plastic chairs beside a bomb-scarred house that served temporarily as a hospital. Just for a chat, he had been told. Just to see if he needed help, to see if he could *be* helped.

"It must be so difficult," said the man, whose face was serene, "to wake up one morning and see that life as you knew it has ended, that so much has been destroyed."

Despite his youth, Younis sensed immediately that the man was trying to get him to do something dangerous. His first instinct was to play it off, to make a grim joke of it—the house was getting old anyway; destruction as a form of camouflage; at least now we don't have to maintain the roof—anything to deflect the course of the inquiry.

But this would not do, he sensed, not with this man who

sat across from him, this friendly man with his placid, expectant face. So how to answer?

Should he talk about his shaking hands, his trembling limbs, the ringing sound in his ear, his blurred vision? Should he describe his physical injuries, show him his wounds, the rudimentary stitches, now nearly ready to be removed, underneath the bandage on his forearm? Should he discuss the numerous times, after he fled into the mountains surrounding the village, that he stood at the cliff edge, wind rushing up into his face, and nearly felt himself take a step off, unconcerned whether he fell or flew?

Or should he talk about—and this was what he found to be the odd thing—the blessing of it? The surprise of finding himself alive, finding himself connected to life. Should he talk about the days after he ran into the mountains, about feeling surrounded, even in that barren place, by life? About the plants that seemed to vibrate with it? Butterflies and rock mice and ants and caterpillars and snow hare and everything he looked at, even the stones, seemed alive. On the mountain he once came face-to-face with a dark falcon riding low on the thermals, wind whooshing through his feathers, and felt one with him, felt peace, as though just by watching the great bird, just by following his example, he could stretch his arms and lift his feet from the ground.

Or should he say that the thing was now part of him, defined him, founded him, that he could no more describe its effect than he could describe being born?

What is it like to lose everything, they ask. The question

takes various forms, and that day, sitting in plastic chairs beside a shattered house, he developed his one and only response.

"What is it like to lose everything?" asked the man, the stranger who was there to help.

And Younis fixed him with his pale green eyes and said, "What is it like not to?"

2

He has a memory, or thinks he does.

They are on the train, the old colonial line running alongside the river to the capital. He lies on the wooden, time-polished bench and rests his head in his mother's lap. Thinking he is asleep, she has draped a loose muslin cloth over his head to cut the sunlight that flickers at them through the passing trees. They are going to meet someone, his father, he thinks. Every so often the wind puffs through the open windows and billows the soft cloth, startling him with a strobe of sunshine, like the bright end of a run-out movie reel.

On the station platform, they stand under a broad roof, which is supported by riveted metal beams, and the engine whistles out a last burst of steam. When the fog clears, a man stands as though he has been waiting since the station was built. He is dressed strangely, in Western clothes, jeans and a starched button-down shirt. His face is freshly shaven, and he carries a backpack made of rough canvas. He takes something from one of the pockets, a little square parcel, carefully wrapped in brown paper and tied with twine, and hands it to Younis's mother, who tucks it quickly away into her shift. It is this he remembers, this package, this passing of something important between them. He has so many questions—Why is he dressed this way? Why has he shaved off his beard?—but when he turns back to ask, the man has gone, disappeared into the throng outside the station gates.

Other things must have happened. They may have stayed a time in the capital, he and his mother, lodging in a cousin's whitewashed spare room near the bazaar. Maybe they bought figs and lamb for their supper, and sipped sweet tea purchased from a vendor's cart. Perhaps, when they heard the call to prayer in the evening, they wandered over to the turreted mosque, washed their feet, and knelt down on the worn rugs. Surely at some point they took the train back home, up the river and into the low hills. But if they did any of these things, as they must have done, he can remember none of them.

And it is this that makes him suspicious, makes him wonder: Maybe it didn't really happen. His inability to remember large parts of the experience makes him question all of it: the carefully wrapped parcel, the riveted beams on the platform, the clean-shaven man who should have worn a beard. Maybe it is all just something he heard about or read much later, his imagination filling in the details and making it his own, something he saw one time, something from a film.

3

He changes his name on the airplane. Somewhere over the Atlantic he assumes his new identity. The flight attendant hands out white-and-blue landing cards, and he borrows a ballpoint pen from the woman sitting next to him to write out his new name—J-O-N-A-S—in the space provided, right next to the space that gives his age: fifteen. Thus named and dated, he signs the card underneath the paragraph explaining that he waives all his legal rights by doing so—his right to counsel, his right to privacy, his right to oppose deportation. He suspects this will cause trouble; he does it anyway. At customs he will be interrogated for hours, kept in a white room with a veneer-top table and steel folding chairs until someone from the Friends International Assistance Society shows up to bail him out. Or later, at his new school, he will explain to anyone who asks—the math teacher, the English teacher, the assistant principal, the head principal—that legally his new name is a direct translation of his old name, even though he feels intuitively that this is not quite true. He knows that the law and the truth are rarely the same thing.

The plane's motion nauseates him, and in an effort to relieve it, he looks out the Plexiglas oval at the blue void below, the gently curving skyline. Occasionally, he spots an island riding the dark sea, marked by a puff of white cumulus. In the plane, he finds it easy to imagine himself floating between two worlds, two existences, each of them true, but does not yet realize that this is a feeling that will never completely leave him.

The female flight attendant has been joined by a skinny, dark-haired man, and together they wheel the clanking metal food cart down the aisle, passing out foil-covered trays, plastic utensils, and plastic, foil-covered cups of distilled water. The action is polite and efficient. Jonas's meal is chicken and some sort of yellowed rice, which he eats with a voraciousness that seems to embarrass his seatmate, an elderly woman with large eyes and an open face.

The airplane lavatory smells of disinfectant and dry air, and seems to aggravate the ringing in his right ear. A sign on the wall warns him that he may be fined three thousand dollars and sent to jail for damaging or disabling the smoke detector. The notion that a smoke detector might exist in the bathroom of an airplane, much less the impulse to damage or disable it, had not previously entered his mind, but now that it has, he wonders how punishment might be exacted, were he so inclined. He has fifty dollars in his pocket, and a small duffel of clothes in the hold, both of which have been given to him by the society, the combination of which constitutes the entirety of his worldly possessions.

Back in his seat, he looks again at his name, written in block capitals in the demarcated spaces on the landing card, and he underlines it with the borrowed pen. The woman, who is sitting on his left, near his good ear, has fallen asleep. He puts the pen down on the tray table and looks at the long, pale scar running up the dark skin on the back of his arm and under his rolled-up shirtsleeve.

"Where did you get that," the woman beside him had asked.

"I fell off a mountain," he had said.

He is beginning to feel claustrophobic in the sealed, pressurized tube. He is tall, constantly mistaken for being older than he is, and his knees knock into the back of the seat in front of him. He can't get comfortable, can't stretch out, and for a moment he fights off a wave of panic. He is surrounded by plastic and metal, which confine him to a predetermined form, a standard that does not comfortably fit him. He pushes his knees again into the back of the seat in front of him, and its occupant shifts, pushing back against him in a kind of warning.

Eventually, a bell dings, and he feels a sinking sensation in his stomach and legs as the plane begins its descent. He fights off another wave of nausea as he folds up his tray table and is told by two different flight attendants to incline his seat. He explains, in nearly panicky tones, that it is broken and that it will not incline, and after this explanation he is left alone.

The ground rises up to meet him, and he feels himself jolted forward, pushes himself into the back of his chair as the plane slows forcefully. When the plane turns from the runway, the gently rolling landscape scrolls past his window like a diorama. How lush, how green it looks! Ivy climbing the massive, broadleafed trees, the atmosphere so thick with humidity that he can see it. And then before he realizes, the plane has rolled up to the gate, and there is a rush for the overhead luggage, and a wafting of heavy, wet air as the door is opened, and they are in the aisles, pushing forward, and he has trouble getting his feet underneath him, trips on a blanket someone has left on the floor, grabs a seat back for support, and it is happening so fast he can't believe it, and he stumbles off the plane and into his new world.

4

The last time he saw his village he was five thousand feet above it.

Sometimes it comes back to him at a word, or a sound, or a scent, and he can see the faint trace of smoke rising toward him like a prayer. From this height he can see the village's broken shell, its careful, jigsaw delineations—yards and orchards and streets—scratched and blurred like a sand castle set upon by a toddler.

Paul tells him that he tends to dissociate.

Jonas goes to see Paul once a week, as he has done since the high school became concerned that he might have been suffering from the results of something traumatic, something they couldn't handle. They suggested that he go see Paul because Paul was someone who knew about these things. Paul had experience. Paul could help him.

Actually, it was slightly more than a suggestion. "We can get a court order," they said, "but we prefer you go voluntarily."

They have been meeting regularly ever since.

During these meetings, they talk about the state of his mental health, which Paul has called, on more than one occasion, "pretty good." Paul has bushy hair and a goatee, and he looks a little bit like a young Karl Marx, an effect amplified by his tendency to explain things in the somewhat dry tones of an economics professor.

"Dissociation is a normal reaction," says Paul. "It's a defense mechanism. And given the circumstances, a certain amount of mental decompensation is probably also to be expected." Paul doesn't seem to understand that this is gibberish until that fact is pointed out to him, and when it is, he tries to make a simplified explanation.

"I know it can feel like touching a hot stove," he says. "Your reflex is to pull your hand away. Your psyche is trying to stem the pain. But to deal with it, to get past it, eventually you are going to have to leave your hand on the stove awhile."

On his desk, Paul has a little silver statue on a marble base. It has sort of a funny shape which is hard to describe, like a wave or an ellipse. Paul tells Jonas that this statue may be used as a focal point, a device to bring him back to the present. It doesn't have to be the statue, he says. It could be anything: a candle, a piece of wood, a lamp, a ball or knickknack, anything, really, but he likes to use this statue because its shape is open to interpretation.

"You are here now," says Paul. "The past is gone, done. Your memories can't physically hurt you. But we need to explore them. We need to understand what happened."

And then they talk.

5

He remembers a conversation, a lecture, voices mixing with the flycatcher's song in the bright courtyard, and his father's friend, the imam, standing tall over him while the early morning sun casts their shadows long over the grass-lined path.

"Now you say it, Younis: 'There is no god but God, and Muhammad is His messenger."

"There is no god but . . ."

"Yes. But God, and . . ."

"But why must I say it?"

"Because this is how you become one of the people. A believer."

"Oh. All right. There is no god but . . ."

"Yes."

"But why must I become one of the people?"

"You must become a believer. We are all believers. Your mother, your father. You come from a long line of believers. Now say it, and when you do so, say it earnestly."

"There is no god but . . ."

"Yes, Younis, you may continue. But God. Please."

"But is it really necessary to say it? Can I not be a believer without doing so? Can I simply think it?"

"It is absolutely necessary. You cannot be a believer without reciting the Kalimah. Now please, Younis, continue."

"There is no god but . . ."

"Yes, Younis, please continue."

"But what if I were mute?"

6

He lives with a host family in a large subdivision outside the city. The Martins. Mr. and Mrs. Martin and their two children, whose names Jonas has trouble pronouncing. The girl is called Courtney, although much to her annoyance Jonas usually drops out the n and compresses the vowel sounds, pronouncing her name so that it sounds much like "Cutie." The boy is Addison, which Jonas pronounces "Ad-son."

The evening Jonas arrives in America, he and the Martins eat dinner together. Mrs. Martin has prepared a pair of large roast chickens, each bigger than any chicken Jonas has ever seen, with light brown gravy and golden roasted potatoes and green beans (which have been steamed, she explains, not boiled, because steaming keeps in more of the vitamins) and glazed carrots and warm bread. The five of them sit around the long table in the dining room stacked with crystal and china and silver on what Mrs. Martin calls a "propitious occasion." Cutie and Ad-son sit across from Jonas, and Mr. and Mrs. Martin sit at either end of the table. Mr. Martin says grace.

"Bless this food to our use," he says. While he continues with the prayer, Jonas glances up anxiously to see that Cutie, her head bowed, is snickering, and then Ad-son flinches as though he has been punched or kicked under the table. Mrs. Martin glares at her children, who hastily compose themselves into a picture of reverence.

"And us to thine service," says Mr. Martin.

After grace, Mrs. Martin tells Jonas that they try to eat dinner as a family every night, but that it's difficult, with the children's after-school activities and other interests, and Mr. Martin's frequent need to stay late at the office. She says that they are making a renewed effort to gather together at the end of each day. She says that this is one of the problems confronting American society, the breakdown of the family, the lack of time families spend together, and that they are trying to counter that trend, but that it's difficult, because they are all so busy with other things. She tells Jonas that, aside from their meals in the evenings, the only thing they do consistently as a family is attend church on Sunday mornings, after which, during the season, they try to get back home in time to watch football on television.

"Do you like football?" asks Ad-son, trying to make eye contact with Jonas over the table.

But Jonas is barely aware of it. His mouth had begun watering almost as soon as he walked in the Martins' front door, and the smell of the roasting meat has tortured him for hours, first as they showed him around the massive house, explaining where his bathroom was and how the taps in the shower worked, because they were new and a little bit tricky, and then when they left him alone in his room, a clean, spare room with a single bed, for nearly an hour, where he was supposed to, he

didn't know, unpack his meager duffel or make himself comfortable or something. But all he could think about was the
food being prepared downstairs.

And so it is some time before he realizes that he has been
asked a question.

Jonas becomes aware that the dining room is silent save for
his own snuffles and grunts. He has ripped off a large chunk
of bread and, together with a slab of chicken breast and half
a potato, grasps it all together in his hand, the silver cutlery
lying untouched on either side of his dinner plate. His mouth
is stuffed full and he wipes a dribble of juice from his chin with
the back of his hand. As he becomes aware of the silence, he
glances up to see that the Martins have not yet begun eating,
but that they are instead all looking at him, staring at him with
expressions that range from fascination to pity to disgust, staring at him as though they have just discovered that they are
sharing their table with some fierce and alien creature.

7

"Where do you go in your mind?" asks Paul.

Jonas watches his reflection in the silver statue on Paul's
desk, leans left and then right to watch his distorted image
play in the light. Jonas feels uncomfortable, examined. In an
effort to deflect the course of the conversation, he talks for
ten minutes about football. American football, which he has
found entirely inescapable on television, a weekly tyranny, he

calls it. But despite his reservations, he has finally given in and started watching it. He draws contrasts with football as the rest of the world knows it, which, Jonas points out, is actually played with the feet.

"Unless you're a goalie," says Paul, to which Jonas half-heartedly agrees.

Paul has laid out some ground rules. He has given Jonas some forms to fill out, asked some general questions, some of which Jonas has answered, and some of which he has not. He has told Jonas that when they meet, they are in a safe space, that they can talk about anything he wants, that he may feel anger and rage and that that's okay, that part of their purpose is to allow him to access those emotions. He has told Jonas that he is legally obligated to report certain crimes, murder, abuse, but that this is for his own protection.

And he has warned Jonas that any hint of physical violence will not be tolerated, that it will instantly end their meetings, and might even lead to jail.

Then he asks Jonas if he has any questions. Paul looks up from his desk to see that Jonas is staring out the window.

"Where do you go in your mind?" asks Paul.

For a time, Jonas says nothing. He looks around the room, back out the window, at the statue on the desk, at the floor. He avoids Paul's gaze for as long as he is able, trying to think of something to say. Then he has a flash. He latches onto an image from his childhood, a glimpse of a thought which seems to him entirely innocuous, and which has suddenly caught in his mind like a shiny pebble.

"Very well," he says at last, "if you really want to know."

8

Another memory. Heat. Sunlight pours through the open windows and into the irregularly shaped schoolroom, where he is gathered with the other students around the long, thick-grained table set to one end. He draws a picture of a lion on the single sheet of lined paper lying before him on the table. The headmaster is speaking in English, but it is a halting, pidgin English, a distant cousin to the flowing, facile language he listens to on the radio, or practices with his father.

("Where did you learn to speak it," he had once asked after an impromptu lesson, out by the well in the courtyard.

"Bradford," his father had said.)

By contrast, the headmaster's only apparent exposure to a native speaker of English seemed to come from his witnessing, as a young man, a crown customs officer adjudicate an impromptu divorce, an anecdote he repeated often, using it to illustrate both his own superior linguistic abilities and the amorality of the colonialist crown. At some point during the divorce proceedings, one of the parties must have uttered the word "insolent," because this is the headmaster's favorite word to use when describing his pupils. As in, "I tolerate no insolence from any of you," or, "Stop your insolent ways," or occasionally, almost randomly, simply uttered to no one in particular, "Insolent."

The headmaster paces the room, looking at each of them

in turn, and then he notices that one pair of eyes is not turned to meet his.

"What is it upon which you work?" says the headmaster. But the words wash over Younis like a breeze. The lion's mane is coming together on the page in front of him, and with only a few more strokes, a couple of precise pencil lines, he is convinced that he will have the perfect representation of—

Pain. His right ear is grabbed, yanked, twisted, a hard grip on his earlobe, and he suddenly understands that what the headmaster lacks in facility with the English language he more than makes up for in his willingness to swiftly issue corporal punishment.

"I said," says the headmaster, "what is that upon which you work?"

"Ah," says Younis, thinking as quickly as he is able while being lifted bodily from his chair by the ear. "Ah . . . but you did not speak to me!"

At this the headmaster pauses, ever so slightly, reducing incrementally the grip on his ear.

"What?" he says.

"You did not speak to me," says Younis, squinting his eye and resisting the urge to slap at the headmaster's hand, an act he knows will result only in the implementation of more brutal measures. "At least, you did not speak to me directly."

"I did, you insolent boy," says the headmaster, renewing his grip. "I ask you upon what it is you work, and now I see it is upon silly doodlings."

"Yes," says Younis, "but you used the collective 'you.'"

"The what?"

"The collective 'you.' The 'you' you used was us. All of us."
Younis tries to motion, or nod, or make some kind of gesture
that would indicate the inclusion of his classmates, now gaping
at the proceedings at the far end of the table, but can only roll
his eyes around the room. The vise on his ear relaxes slightly,
but the grip is not completely released. He realizes he must
keep talking. He takes a breath. "When in a group situation,
as we have here, it is necessary for the speaker, that is you,
if speaking to only one member of the group, to identify the
individual to whom he speaks by name or other moniker, so as
to avoid confusion."

The headmaster's eyebrows knit together, as though of their
own will, making his face look, thinks Younis, not unlike that
of a confused puppy. The grip on his ear relaxing still further,
Younis keeps talking.

"It's one of the basic grammatical rules of the English language," he says.

Too late, he realizes that he has gone too far. A brief flash of
pain shocks his head, this time on his left ear as the headmaster smacks his face. But then it is over.

"Insolent child," says the headmaster as he paces to the
front of the schoolroom. "Insolent, unruly boy."

9

He knows little about his new home. The city's name is abbre-
viated to PIT on the luggage tag that still hangs, six months

after his arrival, from the strap on his duffel, and sounds German to his ear. He imagines it printed in the fractured typeface of old German newspapers. He has seen photos, read some literature. The city is silver, surrounded by water and traversed by bridges. It is home to industry and a sports team whose name sounds familiar, from newspaper articles or radio broadcasts. The society, which has placed him with the Martins, has also enrolled him in a high school, and in a few years can maybe even help him get into the university.

According to a teacher, he lives in the middle of the "rust belt." When he hears the term (which he finds misleading), he pictures himself buckling a flaking iron hoop around his waist. But there is a lot of green space, especially in the suburbs, and the downtown is stainless and tall, but relatively clean, which he is told it did not used to be. Its three rivers, each of them larger than the river next to which he spent his childhood, both bisect and hem in the city. He imagines the boundaries formed by their junction forcing the village, then the town, then the city to grow up rather than out. Underneath the polish is the old city, stone and brick and corniced, pre-Depression confident. Clapboard houses, miners' and steelworkers' houses, lie as though tossed like so many dice onto the surrounding hills, and the university with its towering cathedral looks on from the east.

He strives to adapt to his new life, to understand his place in it. As a welcome present, Mrs. Martin gives him an ornate, leather-bound copy of the Bible, which he keeps on a shelf in his room. For a time, it is his only book.

At the high school, he tries to talk to other students, but they trick him into saying things.

"Hey, Apu," says one of them, blond-haired and cold-eyed, "say, 'Welcome to Quickie Mart.' Say, 'Thank you, come again.'"

He tries to rid himself of the accent, practicing for hours in front of a mirror, but it is hard-wearing, like stone, a singsong abomination.

He gets A's in everything.

He wanders the halls like a ghost.

10

"Where do you go in your mind?" Paul asks. He wants to explore this. Jonas has told him that often he sees his body, his surroundings, and himself from the outside, objectively. This does not happen all the time, only when he is in a particularly high state of stress or concentration, but that when it does he knows what people are thinking, can feel the energy vibrations in a room, and understands hidden meanings. (Later, when Paul mentions that he is privately skeptical of the existence of God, Jonas says, as mysteriously as he can manage: "Yes. I know.")

11

If he remembers anything, he remembers the book.

He remembers the scratching sound of pencil on paper. He remembers wondering, offhandedly at first, but with ever-increasing interest, what was being written. He remembers the compulsion, the care with which the book was usually guarded.

And he remembers spotting it almost by accident, unaccountably left lying on the ground next to the camouflage backpack, as though it had been casually tossed or dropped in the dust, the color of which nearly matched its worn leather cover, obscuring it to the point that he might easily have missed seeing it in the meek dawn.

Alone for the moment, he glances around, then stoops to pick it up. The leather is creased at the spine, bent and folded over at the corners, worn bare at the edges. It feels dense in his hands. A leather tie wraps the book at its middle, and he gently tugs open the precise knot that holds it closed.

The inside cover is inscribed with a compass rose, next to which is a brief, handwritten dedication in flowing script. The journal is filled with long stretches of text, each separated by half a blank page. Some sections take up multiple pages; some are only one or two paragraphs long. For the most part, the writing is a slanted, hasty scrawl, but occasionally it refracts into neat printing. Penciled-in scratch marks and corrections fill the margins.

He is able to read only the first page. Before he gets a chance to go any further, he hears rocks clattering outside the cave mouth, and realizes the soldier has returned. He quickly closes the book, hastily ties the leather strap with a knot that faintly imitates the original, and puts the book back on the ground next to the pack.

Eventually, he will read the whole thing. At first he will read with passing interest, and then with increasing fascination, and finally with dread. After he reads it, unsure what to do next, he will take the book to the back of the cave and wedge it underneath some rocks, confident that he is the only one who will ever be able to find it again.

But for now, the fear of being discovered forces him to be content with stolen glances and skimmed passages. He knows he is trespassing, that these words were not meant for him. But he is able to convince himself that if he proceeds carefully, respectfully, he will harm nothing, violate no sacred laws. He is allowed to read it, he reasons, because he needs to know whom he is dealing with.

12

You deserve an explanation.

I have had this book with me ever since you gave it to me on my eighteenth birthday. During all that time I have not scratched a hundred words into it. Countless times I have thought of packing it away, or misplacing it, or leaving it behind somewhere. But I kept it. Maybe this is why.

I won't try to justify anything we did, but you should know what happened. Maybe you will read something in the paper. Or maybe you will see a reporter talking into a microphone in the dusty aftermath. Maybe you will think to yourself that the snowy mountains behind him would be beautiful in another context. By then, it will be done. It will feel historical, like a stock-market crash or an election. It will seem inevitable.

But this was not inevitable. We did exactly what we were supposed to do. Maybe that's the horror of it. To call it an accident would be false. To call it a mistake implies that it was unintentional.

What we did stank of intention.

13

"Welcome to America," they say.

It is said often during the two years he stays with the Martins at their large home in the suburbs. They first said it to him when he arrived at their house on a muggy summer afternoon, the duffel slung over his shoulder as he crossed the threshold into a cavernous foyer and a cold blast of conditioned air.

"Welcome to America," they said.

But since then, he is welcomed to America regularly. It becomes a kind of joke.

They say, "Welcome to America," when he expresses astonishment at how friendly everyone is, smiling at him every time he opens his mouth to say anything, smiling at his accent. He is welcomed to America when he comments on the number of church steeples visible in the city and the surrounding towns. He is welcomed to America when he mentions the number of hours the Martins spend sitting passively in front of their television set.

He is welcomed to America when he makes the mistake of saying that he does not like American football, which is all but a second religion in the Martin household. But Jonas says that it's a jerky, start-stop kind of game that lacks rhythm and grace and beauty. He is welcomed to America when the family goes out for fast food one night (slumming it, they call it), and they laugh as Jonas wolfs down four double cheeseburgers in rapid succession, then express concern ("You really think he's okay?") as he spends half an hour vomiting audibly in the bathroom.

He is welcomed to America when he makes any of thousands of observations about his new world: the largeness of the cars, the tallness of the buildings, the neatness of the manicured lawns, the cleanliness of the parks, the skimpiness of the girls' clothing, the enormity of the meals served at restaurants.

For a short time, the Martins welcome him to America anytime he says anything.

One evening Jonas and the Martins walk down Stanwix Street together after a lavish dinner at the Chatham Center, Jonas having eaten triple portions of a succulent roast served from the buffet. A dark figure sits in a doorway off of the sidewalk, legs splayed out in front of him, rattling a paper cup with a few coins in it. As he has done with the past three such figures they have passed on the street, Mr. Martin pulls a bill out of his wallet and gives it to Jonas to drop into the man's cup.

"Thank you, sir," says the man.

"You are welcome," says Jonas, suddenly uncomfortable.

"Hey," says the man, "you have a funny accent!"

"Yes," says Jonas.

"Well," says the man, "welcome to America."

14

He remembers that they first came to see him while he was still in the hospital. It was run by Americans, and he remembers the bright light filtering into his room through curtains as clean and white as the fresh bandages wrapped around his forearm. He was hooked up to a tube that they said would keep him hydrated, and there was a little vase of flowers on a table next to the bed, brought to him by a smiling army nurse in a white uniform, who told him only that the flowers had been sent by friends.

They expressed keener interest in him after they learned he could speak English. He told them he learned it in school, that his father spoke it fluently, that he always listened to the BBC, that he loved American movies.

But good as his English was, he had trouble understanding their questions. It seemed they asked him his name hundreds of times, so often that he started giving them different names each time they asked. "No, you must be mistaken; I am Raul," he would say, or, "I'm sorry, Younis is no longer here. I am Klaus."

They took it as a sign of spirit.

Their questions increased in number and meandered aimlessly, so he simply chatted with them, digressing at will. He chatted amiably about the time of day, the date, the color of the sky, the best way to make couscous, the history of central Asia, animal husbandry, the legends of the constellations, methods to determine whether someone was lying, tips for negotiating with sellers in the market. On these subjects and others he seemed to impress them with his knowledge, or, absent knowledge, his ability to substitute plausible conjecture.

But when they would ask, as they periodically did, about his family, his mother, at least, or his father, the English speaker, for whom they were searching diligently, or his home, so they might better know where to search, he fell silent, studying with rapt attention the coarse weave of the cotton blankets, and refused to speak. They insisted that they were searching everywhere, and that anything he could tell them would be helpful. They pleaded with his silence, but eventually their pleas gave way to the realization, faint at first, but growing with each passing day, that perhaps he remained silent because he knew they would never be found.

Jonas finds the Martin children to be a mystery.

Ad-son is a mystery because Jonas rarely sees him. He is the same age as Jonas, and he appears briefly before school, for breakfast, and occasionally at dinner before he disappears into his room for hours on end. Once in a while he says something to Jonas, asks him a question about video games or sports, but these questions are posed in passing. Ad-son seems to remain uninvested in Jonas, unemotional, as though by speaking with him, he is utilizing the scientific method to query a science experiment.

Cutie is a mystery because Jonas does not see her enough. She is two years older, and heavily involved in school activities, cheerleading and gymnastics and something called pep club. Jonas is shocked to find that the Martins allow her to visit with her boyfriend in the living room entirely unsupervised. He is alternately attracted to her and repelled by her, forcing himself not to dwell upon her bare legs or the occasional swear word that escapes her lips when she thinks her parents aren't listening. For a time, he is vaguely concerned about living with a family that allows their only daughter to be alone with a man who is not a blood relative, particularly while wearing such provocative clothing.

Cutie, in turn, seems to regard Jonas with an affectionate, condescending interest, as though he is a puppy that has wandered into her garden. After breakfast one morning, she kisses her mother on the cheek, punches Ad-son in the arm, and then pats Jonas on the head before gliding through the house and out the front door to her boyfriend's waiting car, carried on a cloud of perfume and a toss of blond hair.

Once, when everyone has left the house, he stands in turn at each of the doorways to their bedrooms and tries to place them into context. He does not enter the rooms, in part out of fear of being caught, and in part out of fear of what he might find.

Cutie's room is pink and white, the corners piled with dirty clothes and the shelves punctuated with a smattering of toys left over from a time when she was a younger girl: stuffed animals, a doll or a glittery pinwheel or knickknacks held firm like memories.

Ad-son's room is tidier, but is still filled with stuff, with superheroes and army men, a computer screen on a desk in front of the window, at which he sits for hours a day in front of video games and other mysteries. The walls of both rooms are covered with posters—singers and actors in Cutie's room, and in Ad-son's, football and hockey players and, on the wall next to his desk, a tiny picture of a girl in a bathing suit.

By contrast, Jonas's room is austere, bare-walled, with a simple pine table and chair, both of them labeled with stickers underneath that say, "IKEA," and a small closet, which is empty except for Jonas's several hanging shirts.

"You can change things around however you like," Mrs. Martin had said when she first showed him the room. "We can take you to get some things."

It was said almost in passing, in the midst of the activity

surrounding his arrival, but then the weeks had rolled by, and the promise to "get some things" for the room had been forgotten. Jonas doesn't mind, though. For one thing, he likes the room's clean spareness, and feels that within its space his existence is boiled down to its most basic essence, devoid of the complications of ownership and maintenance.

But the main reason he does not decorate his room is that he feels it would make him too familiar.

Like their rooms, the Martin children announce their identities to the world, inform everyone who cares to know about their every want, dream, proclivity, interest, hobby, or passion. Within a few months, Jonas feels that he knows basically everything there is to know about their lives. For example, he knows that Cutie, although superficially warm and friendly, values her popularity and standing at school above almost anything else, that her greatest fear is losing her status. He knows that Ad-son, while trying to appear cool and aloof and smart, is concerned about where he fits in, about the prospect of living forever in his sister's shadow.

But Jonas lives in a clean white room with a single bed. He strives to keep himself unknowable. He comes to see mystery as an asset. For as much a mystery as he once found the Martin children, he himself remains a far deeper mystery. He enjoys being unfamiliar. Exotic. But he fails to realize that, by declining the opportunity to define himself, he allows others, less interested, more callous, meaner others, to create definitions for him.

16

"Where do you go in your mind?" asks Paul, and Jonas tells him that sometimes he doesn't know, that sometimes he looks up to realize that an hour or more has passed as he sits in the library, or on the edge of his bed, or on a park bench, and that he has no recollection of it.

"Doesn't that worry you?" asks Paul. "How much time do you spend in this way, drifting and unaware, in your head?"

At first Jonas doesn't understand the question. Or thinks that maybe he understands it differently from the way Paul intends it. But then he thinks that he does understand, and his face lights up with comprehension.

"Oh, lifetimes," he says at last. "I have spent lifetimes unconscious."

17

Reluctantly, Jonas remembers that the soldier was called Christopher. When he eventually says the name, he pronounces it precisely, unaccented, as though he has practiced saying it.

"I probably would not have survived without him," says Jonas, looking around the office, out the window, searching for something interesting to comment upon, something to once

again shift the conversation. They have been circling this subject for twenty minutes, Paul pushing him for more information, and Jonas reluctant to talk about it.

"Is it not enough," says Jonas, "to know that I have been
helped by many people?"

"Why won't you talk about him?"

"There was a doctor," says Jonas. "At the American hospital. She was older than myself, but still young, for a doctor. Let
us talk about her. She was wonderful. She helped me. She had
smooth hands and fine wrinkles around her eyes, from laughing, and for the time I was there I lived on her smile."

"And yet you can talk about her easily."

"She helped me. I probably wouldn't be here without her,
either."

"But you recall her without difficulty. While this other person,
this Christopher, you do not like to mention him. Why is this?"

"She was prettier."

When Paul does not respond, but simply looks levelly at
Jonas from across his desk, Jonas says, "Is it not enough to
know that I survived, that I have been helped along the way?"

"I'm afraid," says Paul, "that it is not."

18

I am no longer certain of much.

I carry a stone around in my pocket. It's hard gray granite. It is pierced by a thin, marbled vein of white quartz. I can feel its rough surface on my palm, but I am consumed by the fear that it will turn to dust in my hand.

Increasingly, I find everything I cling to is fragile.

I remember from an earth sciences class that the white quartz in the stone was formed by something called an igneous intrusion. A crack in the granite let a tiny thread of magma, under pressure, penetrate the rock, where it cooled for years, eventually turning into the white streak running through the gray stone. The streak is like a scar, the molten rock pressed into it like blood.

This is not a rare occurrence, this penetration of solid rock by molten rock under pressure. It happens all the time. Deep in the earth, it is happening right now. Stones like this are not scarce. Just yesterday I walked through a field littered with them. An entire field full of scarred stones. They are abundant. For every diamond in the ground there are probably a million stones like this one. And yet to me, right now, it is the most beautiful thing in the world. The invasion, the pressure. The magma has exploited the injured rock, and has made it beautiful.

When I lie here and cannot sleep, these are the sorts of things I tell myself.

19

Outdoors, Jonas is in charge, at peace. It's late summer, early September, and he walks slowly, reluctantly to school, out of the subdivision and into the lush forest that encroaches from all sides, the sights and smells as if from a tropical island, compared with the desert hills of his childhood. He memorizes their names: the musky scent of Bradford pear, the earthy sassafras, the brilliant rhododendron. Autumn is filled with the deep mystery of fallen leaves, the first sharp whiff of coming frost, lit by curious jack-o'-lanterns, and the winter, foot after foot of snow.

He reads the Bible he has been given. He reads that God created light and darkness on the first day, then that He created the sun, which separates day and night, on the fourth. He reads that man was created before woman, then that they were created at the same time. He reads that God is jealous, and then that He is loving and kind; that man is inherently evil, and then that he is created in God's image; that woman is equal to man, and then that she is subservient. He strives to find in it some direction, some solace from the Book's words, some sense of comfort, but he is instead driven mad by its internal inconsistencies.

The taunting turns physical. Jonas's skinny frame persuades some of the bolder kids that he won't fight back. It's relatively mild at first: stepping on his heels in the hallway to pull off his shoes, overturned plates of food, and when Jonas tells them to stop they just laugh harder.

"Say it again, Apu. 'Stop eet.'"

He shows up late to class. Sometimes he doesn't show up. He finds the schoolwork almost ridiculously easy, and reasons that it is deserving of only part of his time. He spends a whole day in a wooded trace of land between home and school, sitting under a sugar maple. He tracks a deer for a mile in the forest.

The next day he shows up to school as though nothing happened, and the senile old teacher asks for a written excuse, signed by his host parents.

"What excuse," he says, "I was here."

She walks away, looking confused.

Even attending part-time, he gets A's.

20

Where do you go in your mind, Paul asks, and Jonas tells him that sometimes he travels to a meadow with a clear stream running through the middle of it, past a shade tree where a lioness and a gazelle stand looking at each other, a cobalt sky spread overhead. This place is the result of a creativity exercise that was once taught to him by a writing teacher. It was supposed to be a safe place where they could access their inner voice, their muse, but he's not sure that's exactly what it turned out to be.

"It is a mental construct," he says to Paul. "I know it is not real."

21

There is much he cannot remember. In place of these memories, his head is filled with facts. Names, dates, places. He
is baffled by what he knows almost as much as by what he
does not. For example, he knows that the Empire State Building is nearly fifteen hundred feet tall, that the Declaration
of Independence was written in 1776, that the New Deal
saved America from communism, that the first World Series
was played in 1903. These facts were given to him by the 1980
edition of *The New Book of Knowledge* encyclopedia, which
showed up, minus the V volume, in an aid shipment, or maybe
with a missionary group, and sat with a smattering of other
books—a large English dictionary, the Koran, *A Tale of Two
Cities*—in a rough-hewn bookcase at the back of the schoolroom, its row of blue-and-white spines promising enlighten-
ment.

He remembers staying after class to read it, volume by
volume, turning the pages right to left as the late-afternoon
sunlight slanted through the school window. New York was
founded by the Dutch; Gutenberg invented the printing press;
the American Civil War was fought to end slavery.

But he is nagged by the suspicion that his brain space is
limited, that his mind must toss some things over into the current so that others might be accommodated. It is as though
he has exchanged memories for facts, as though whole periods

of his childhood have been replaced by lists of questionably useful trivia.

The California gold rush began in 1848; Rosa Parks refused to give up her bus seat; William the Conquerer conquered England; the Mormons founded Utah.

22

The school day begins with a half-hour period known as "homeroom."

It is the period Jonas dreads.

He sits at one corner of the large, desk-filled classroom, as far from the other students as he can get, and prays not to be called upon or otherwise prompted to interact. In the space of only weeks, he has come to fear this half hour more than any other time of the day, an aimless gathering of teenagers that can turn predatory in an instant. The homeroom teacher is an old woman who can barely control her hormone-fueled students. She frequently leaves the room on one ill-timed errand or another, and when she comes back, she seems not to register the hurriedly hushed chaos that has descended in her absence.

Already, Jonas has become a target. He barely comprehends how it happened. The quizzical looks he receives when he says anything, his unusual phrases, his dark complexion, his worn clothes, and then, one morning, the wet splat of a spitball that sticks to his cheek, a hollow ballpoint pen hurriedly tucked out of sight, the muffled snickers of all who witnessed it, and suddenly he has become the outlet for all of homeroom's pent-up aggression.

One day someone invents a game, the object being to see who can hit Jonas with the most spitballs during the brief time the teacher is absent from the room.

Every morning, he sits at his corner desk and remains quiet. He tries to blend into the wall, the Formica desktop, the floor. He attempts to render himself invisible.

And then the old teacher steps out of the room again, and almost instantly Jonas is grabbed from behind, his arms pinned to his sides. A boy's face appears in front of his, freckled and smiling, puckers his lips, and for a horrified instant, Jonas fears he is about to be kissed. And then Jonas feels a long stream of thick spittle running down his cheek. Someone else, someone unseen, spits at him again, but misses his face, and he feels it lodge instead in his hair.

He hears a girl's voice say, "Eww, stop it; that's gross," but his arms remain pinned to his sides. And then, straining, he breaks free of the grip and stands up, his face wet and smelling of other people's mouths. At that moment the old teacher steps back into the room, sees him standing up at his desk, and tells him sharply to sit back down.

"Welcome to America," someone whispers, and the room erupts into laughter.

23

He remembers talking with one of his sponsors, just after he arrived in America. He remembers asking her why they were helping him.

"We are the right hand," she said.

She was the director of the Friends International Assistance Society, the Quaker organization that helped people like him. She was heavyset and wore thick glasses, and she had a kindly face, but tired, her soft brown eyes deep and compassionate. She had just given him the small allowance he could use for "incidental expenses," as they were called, which at this time usually consisted of pizza and bottomless cups of cola. He would meet with her regularly, every few weeks, and she would inquire after his progress, his health, his social adjustment. She would ask about his host family, which the society had found through an interfaith cooperative, and his school, his classes, his friends. He always painted for her a pleasant, sanitized picture, because he felt it would be rude to do otherwise.

He remembers her handing him this little sum of money sealed in a tiny white envelope, and he asked her why she did it, why she helped people like him. She looked at him for a moment from across her cheap metal desk, and then she said, "We are the right hand."

This confused him. "The right hand of what?" he asked. "God?" He was amazed, because this was the kind of thing only zealots thought highly enough of themselves to say, and this woman was no zealot. But she laughed gently.

"No, nothing so bold." She glanced out the window briefly, as though looking for permission to continue; then she looked back to him. "Unfortunately," she said, "our country sometimes has a habit of making a mess with its left hand and cleaning it up with its right. We are the right hand."

24

The kid saved me. I should probably make that point. He showed me the way out. I saw him running down the street out of the corner of my eye, and out of habit I lifted my weapon toward him. I saw that he was running away from me, and I looked around, at what we had just done, and I saw this kid run down an alley, and I followed him. It wasn't logical. There was no reason in it. He could have been leading me anywhere, death trap or salvation, and I didn't care which. You always have choices, but there are times when the split second before you is so starkly illuminated, it becomes clear that everything you are, and everything you are ever going to be, hangs in the balance. And I had one choice to make, which is basically the choice you always have to make in any situation: stay or go.

So I went. I followed him. I didn't care where he led me. And he ducked between some houses and down to the river, and then north along the river. I stayed far enough back that he didn't know I was there, which was pretty easy, because the moonlight seemed to shine on everything, and I could see him clearly up ahead of me, and the noise from the river, wide and beautiful and cursed, drowned out everything else.

25

They share a conversation in the kitchen, in the suburbs, Cutie and Ad-son clearing up after dinner, the clinking of plates and glasses in the sink, the canned echo of laughter from the television in the family room, the low hum of the dishwasher, and Mrs. Martin sitting alone with him at one corner of the kitchen table.

"I'd like to talk to you about something, Jonas," she says, and for a moment he suspects she is on the verge of reaching out to grasp his hand. "Something important."

"Okay."

"You have traveled a long way to come to us, haven't you?"

"Yes."

"And you must have had many difficult experiences. Some horrible things must have happened to you."

"Yes."

"Jonas, did you ever think that perhaps there is a larger plan at work? Did you ever think that maybe you were brought here for a reason?"

"Well, I don't . . . I mean, I'm not sure."

"Jonas, I need to tell you that there is a way to clear away all of these horrible experiences. A way to find comfort. A way to be forgiven for all of your sins."

"Yes, well . . ."

"Jonas, I'm going to ask you probably the most important question you will ever be asked."

"Are you?"

"It's the same question I was asked years ago, the same question Mr. Martin was asked, and our children. We have all done this."

"Okay, but . . ."

"Jonas, will you accept Jesus Christ as your personal Lord and savior?"

"My what?"

"Your personal Lord and savior. Will you establish a personal relationship with Jesus Christ?"

"My . . . savior from what?"

"From your sins, of course."

"My sins?"

"Yes, Jonas. Your sins. After all, we are all sinners in the eyes of the Lord."

"But were we not created in His image?"

"That was before. Before we sinned. Now we are all sinners, and must seek His forgiveness by accepting Jesus, whom He sent to die for us, to cleanse us of our sins."

"All our sins?"

"Yes. But we must accept Him first."

"All the sins of all the world?"

"Yes, Jonas."

"Then he must truly have His hands full."

26

Where do you go in your mind, Paul asks, and Jonas tells him sometimes he travels someplace else. He goes there in his dreams or in his waking thoughts, but when he is there, he is really there. He stands up high on the southern mountain, the wind blasting up from the far valley below, the first glow of sunrise pale in the east. The smoke, now black and ominous, rises from the burning village, and gunshots echo methodically from the rocks. No, Jonas tells him, this place is real. As real as the pen in your hand, as you note it, as real as the paper and ink. As real as that morning when it comes roaring back to him, standing on the precipice, so scared he can't feel a thing.

And then he's back, the poltergeist fading in the rearview mirror of Paul's silver statue, and he's safe, and maybe he understands a little bit more, and maybe he is ever so slightly wiser.

27

He remembers a clear day on the hill overlooking the village. The rapid, light-handed tapping of metal on stone echoing out over the valley as the mason labors beside a freshly dug grave.

The supine stone, destined to join the chorus of standing rocks which either reach for or point to God, is the same shape, but a shade lighter than its neighbors, which have weathered months or years or centuries and darkened accordingly, their rows on the hillside presenting a graded palette of loss.

He remembers staying in the mosque after prayers, kneeling with his eyes closed while everyone else stood to leave.

"Peace be upon you."

"And upon you."

He remembers the entire village weeping, and his father's angry vows of revenge. He remembers feeling as though there were something overhead, a lens or a prism, an inverted pyramid, serving as a conduit, through which all the world's sorrow was focused.

He remembers how they lowered them into the wounded earth, how they could have been sacks of laundry, or wool rugs wrapped in their protective gauze.

He remembers how, despite his vehement wishes, peace didn't come to him through prayers, or reading the Book, or fiery sermons, all of which served only to cloud his focus. So he learned to wait for it. He would stay a long time, waiting. Forever if he had to, kneeling on the mosque's worn rugs, long after everyone else had left, keeping his eyes closed until he lost track of time, forcing himself to stay, to concentrate through boredom and aching knees and legs fallen asleep, until at last it came, entering his soul with a whisper.

28

When he cannot be outdoors, he escapes the bullying, the interminable host family, the simplistic classes, by hiding away in the high school's library. If the rest of the school is institutional, spartan, coldly lit by fluorescent lights, the library is an oasis of wooden bookshelves and learning, as though built a hundred years earlier. At some point, he comes to realize that this is because it was built years earlier, and while the rest of the school has been recently renovated—shiny, stainless-steel laboratory equipment in the science department, new classrooms filled with sparkling plastic-and-Formica-topped desks, whiteboards instead of chalkboards, a new athletics stadium— the library has undergone no such renovation. Unrefurbished as it is, timeworn and outdated though its shelves and tables and massive card-catalog file are, it is the best-appointed library Jonas has ever seen. As soon as he discovers it, almost by accident one afternoon while wandering the halls, he spends all his free time there.

He reads not only the Bible he has been given, but reads about it, about how it was created. He learns about the Council of Nicaea, where, as far as he can tell, a bunch of priests got together and determined, more or less arbitrarily, what would be included in the Book and what would not. He reads about what was not. He reads about the Apocrypha, the Gospel According to Thomas, and Peter and James. He reads about the Nag

Hammadi manuscripts. He is utterly fascinated by the thought that these writings had survived nearly two thousand years buried in the desert, that they had to be buried so that they might survive.

Often it is dark when he leaves the library, his footfalls echoing from the linoleum floor and institutional green tiles of the hallway. He stays so late that he is nearly locked in the building several times, and has to be let out by the scowling janitor. But he thinks to himself that, with so much he does not know, so much reading to do, this might not be so bad, to be sealed inside such a bastion of knowledge overnight, or for a weekend at the very most.

29

The recruiters came and talked with us in school, and I remember it like yesterday. I wasn't interested. I told them I wanted to do something good. I told them I wanted to help people. I told them I couldn't do it, told them I wasn't interested.

But they told me that there was no better way to do good and to help people. They told me they helped people all the time. Doing good was what they were about. Plus they were going to pay me. Where else could I get paid for helping people? Plus they would pay for my college. Plus, in addition to helping people, and paying me, and paying for my college, they would teach me a skill. I would be helping people, and seeing the world, and earning money, and hav-

ing college paid for, and learning a skill that I could use later to earn money and help people.

In the end, it was a pretty easy decision.

30

He makes it into the news twice.

The first time, he is mentioned within a single sentence, in the form of a number. He is one of eighteen injured civilians. Twelve killed, eighteen injured. When she thinks he is old enough, the director of the Friends International Assistance Society tentatively shows him the newspaper clipping, which she has kept for long enough that it is just beginning to yellow at the edges. The article is short, and he has to read it three times before he realizes that he is not reading about someone else. He catches himself feeling that feeling, that momentary luxury of denial, of thinking, Oh, well, at least there were survivors. He is surprised at how little space the story occupies.

Then he wonders which number he was.

"I think that I was number five," he says. "Of the eighteen."

"Why do you think that?"

"It just feels right."

31

He walks down the high school hallway. It's late in the day, after hours, and Jonas has been in the library since the final bell. He has been reading once again about the Bible. He has become obsessed with it.

He has learned that the original son of God, prince of peace, savior of the world, was Caesar Augustus, that these honorifics were bestowed upon him by the Roman senate. This increases Jonas's admiration for the early Christians, for their acts of defiance, appropriating the emperor's titles to their crucified leader, an act that virtually guaranteed their own executions. And even though Mrs. Martin has told him repeatedly that the Book is the inerrant word of God, that it contains only historical facts, the more he learns, the more he comes to believe that the writings themselves live in metaphor, that they seek not to convey factual information, but to reveal larger truths. He comes to believe that by insisting on taking them literally, Mrs. Martin manages to simultaneously denigrate the scriptures and paint herself a fool.

And so he walks down the hallway after hours, considering the meaning of spiritual truth, the enlightened path, and suddenly there is one of them, the big kid with freckles, standing next to the lockers and laughing with several of his friends.

They have been waiting for him.

"Hey, Apu," says the freckled kid, sneering, and shoves Jonas into the bank of lockers, holds his head against the wall, reaches down to try to do something with his underwear.

Jonas is flooded with despair. Something snaps, something in his mind. Whatever has allowed him to remain passive and afraid snaps like a thread. He feels it, feels the change, as his entire body becomes one single, collective muscle.

He lifts his knee hard into the kid's crotch, grabs a finger and pulls it back, yanking his arm, trips him to the ground. The freckle-faced kid becomes an object, a talisman through which Jonas focuses his rage.

He grabs a textbook from the floor and slams it edgewise down into the face, listens to the bridge of the nose snap, watches twin rivulets of blood flow over the mouth, spreading a red stain on the shirt. The freckled kid lies prone on the ground, holding his face, and Jonas stomps on his knee with both feet, jumps on it up and down, over and over, trying desperately to break the leg. The kid's friends struggle to pull Jonas off, but he breaks free and kicks the freckled kid in the head, opening a gash along the top of his skull.

From nowhere a teacher reaches in and, now with the help of the freckled kid's friends, grabs Jonas and holds him down, pinning his outstretched arms to the ground.

He is assigned to the school psychologist. There are concerns about post-traumatic stress.

The next day he goes and talks with her. He is surprised by what they don't know about him, by his constant need to explain himself in a way they might understand.

"Where did you get that scar," she asks, looking at Jonas's arm.

"I once fought a lion," says Jonas, "and he gave me this."

She is not buying it, but doesn't press the issue. Instead, she asks how he feels.

Eventually, she will tell him that he is fascinating to talk to, that she wants to help, but that her field of expertise does not include him, his "situation," she will call it. But she knows someone, someone good, someone experienced, someone Jonas really needs to see.

"Based on what has happened, we can get a court order," she says. "But I prefer you go voluntarily."

And that's when he starts going to see Paul.

But in the meantime, Jonas is happy to sit in her office and chat, and the conversation gets him out of gym class.

32

Another memory, like a faintly recalled dream. He is walking home from somewhere, across the rough, upturned sod, his breath forming the only clouds under the bright sun. As he approaches the house, his mother comes out the back door carrying a jug of tea and an earthenware cup. He vividly remembers that when she pours the tea, two streams come out: the liquid filling the cup, and the steam drifting up in a hazy mirror image, mingling with their breath.

Later, his father arrives, eclipsing the front door's rectangle of light as he stoops to enter it. He is bearded, and wearing his shalwar, and carrying a large duffel. He has fractured memories of a meal, of his father smoking a pipe at the head of the table. They laugh, but it's an uneasy laugh, as though they know that it is all just temporary.

After dinner, his father disappears into the back room. As his mother clears up, he rises from the table and creeps down the brief passageway, past a low, wooden bench, to peek his head around the corner and look into his parents' bedroom. His father is laying his things out on the floor, shirts and belts, and the plump duffel is open and leaning against the wall. In his memory, the interior of the bag glows as though filled with fireflies, but he knows this is a trick of his mind, looking backward, long after he has peered into it and seen that it is filled with money.

"Hey, get out of here, you little thief!" says his father, laughing. But this is where memory plays another trick. For is it a hearty, honest laugh? Does it not contain some hint of apprehension? Of frustration at the broken secrecy? Of irritation? Of anger? Or perhaps even hidden admiration for his son's stealth, entering the room without being noticed?

It is impossible for him to tell, to look back and see clearly, and each attempt he makes to do so, to clarify his memory, sharpen its lines, results only in further blurring the picture, smudging it like a clumsy child playing with finger paints.

33

The second time he makes the news, a reporter phones him after getting wind of his story. The city has apparently become home to a sizable population of "displaced persons," which has temporarily made it the subject of the national news cycle.

"People would be really interested," says the reporter. "How you came here, how you're making a life for yourself." Noting Jonas's reluctance, the reporter tries to generate a certain level of excitement, and ends up sounding like a game-show host when he says, "After all, you're a success story!"

Jonas wants to ask about all the others, the "sizable population." He wants to scream. He wants to tell him to go to hell.

In the end, he hangs up the phone on him, leaving the article to be written using different sources, other people, before referring obliquely to "countless others who live right here in our own area, some of them too traumatized to speak about their experiences."

This time, he doesn't bother wondering which one he is.

34

The fight lends him an air of credibility, of danger. He is suddenly someone not to be fucked with. He learns of another refugee who attends the school, Hakma, a Kurd, who has lived in America since he was two years old. He does not have Jonas's accent, but shares his dark skin and hair, and they hit it off instantly. Hakma does not remember his brief time as an infant in Kurdistan, but injustice suffuses his soul. They pal around, meeting up after school to walk to one or the other's house and sitting conspiratorially across from each other in the cafeteria.

Students begin to talk to him. Girls seem to like him, mostly, he thinks, because he looks so different from the tow-headed boys they usually know. He has sharp features, which he claims are the product of generations spent in the wind and mountains, pale green eyes, and ink black hair. He learns to cultivate an aura of mystery, of danger, hinting at past experiences and feats without ever coming right out and describing them. Some of his classmates think it is all an act, a reputation built on air and a lucky punch, while others are reverential. He is invited to parties, and often, because he looks older, he is able to buy the beer.

His grades fall.

His teachers describe him as well-adjusted.

35

But there are events about which he refuses to speak.

Paul says, "Maybe you can tell me more about that."

Jonas signals his reluctance in one of two ways: either he

talks purposefully about other things, real things, imagined things, or some combination of the two, or else he is silent, fixing his gaze on the floor in front of him and waiting for the subject to shift of its own volition.

"This is important," says Paul.

"Did you know," says Jonas, taking a quick, deep breath, "that as a young boy I met the Dalai Lama?"

"Really," says Paul.

"Really," says Jonas. "A brave man, Mr. Lama. Very brave. For him to travel to our village, as he did. We were not always particularly tolerant of other perspectives. But he came, paying no heed to the potential danger. He stood out, to be sure, in his red-and-yellow robes, and his shaved head. He was a sight, I can tell you.

"It was the planting season, and I was out in the field, as we all were at that time of year. Mr. Lama, he came walking up the road, up from the river. I do not remember, exactly, whether he came by himself, or whether he was accompanied by others. Now that I think about it, though, I realize he must have had others with him, some sort of retinue. There is a fine line between brave and foolhardy, is there not? Mr. Lama would not have traveled to us alone. That would have crossed the line into foolishness.

"But I remember him, not his accompaniment. He walked up the road in his bright robes and his shaved head, walked right out into the freshly turned field, walked until he stood directly in front of me. And he looked down at me and smiled. Then he said something to me that I will never forget."

"Jonas," says Paul.

"He said, 'Just as the seed you sow today will grow to feed

your village, so shall you, my young friend, grow to nourish the world.'"

"Jonas."

"And then he took my hand in his . . ."

"Jonas."

"And he held it, and . . ."

"Jonas, we were talking about the last time you saw your sister alive."

"Yes," says Jonas, fixing a dull gaze somewhere in the space between them. "Yes. Mr. Lama liked her very much, as well."

36

Another memory: It must have been spring, the gullies filled with meltwater, and they have finished supper. His father stands up and strokes his beard, then goes outside, muttering for Younis to follow. There has been talk all winter. Talk of something big happening, some change, or threat, but he is so young, and it is nearly impossible to reconstruct from the scattered clues of memory. They make their way down to the river, his father several steps ahead, and then they turn onto the river road, walking upstream.

"I'm going to show you something," says his father, "and I want you to remember it."

They walk along the packed stone road, and after an hour they take a break, stooping to drink from a shallow pool near the shore. Out in its middle, the river flows savagely, but it is placid along the bank. The tempest out in the center seems to be totally unconnected to the calm water gently lapping the rocks beside their feet, and yet he can watch a stick or a leaf drifting near the shore, suddenly swept up into the rapids, dancing wildly away.

Eventually they come to one large, flat stone balanced on top of another, forming a distinctive, crooked T shape at the edge of the river, the water roaring around the base.

"See that rock?" asks his father over the river's din, pointing. "Remember that rock. Memorize it, so that you will know it when you see it again."

They turn west, away from the river and toward the mountains, white-capped and imposing. When they come to the base of the foothills, the sun is low in the sky, and his father points to a thin path, little more than a faint wear in the stone and dirt, that leads away and straight up the hill, weaving around a large boulder and disappearing into a hollow in the hills.

His father looks up at the half-formed trail and then down at Younis. "Two hours' walk up this path there is a cave," he says. "If anything ever happens, go there." He looks up again at the mountains, impervious and assured and unconcerned. "I will meet you if I can."

37

The letter, when it arrives, is expected. It is in a thick manila envelope that hints at packets of information enclosed, forms

to be filled out and returned. He is happy to receive it, grateful even, but not surprised. Conversations had occurred,
things had been arranged, and he had received a phone call
the week before, explaining, in congratulatory tones, what was
to come.

University of Pittsburgh
Office of Admissions
5413 Fifth Avenue
Pittsburgh, PA 15601

Dear Jonas Iskander,

*We are writing to officially inform you that you
have been awarded the Nelson A. Atkinson scholarship
for the current academic year. As you may know, the
scholarship is awarded annually to an incoming freshman from outside the United States who has, in the
view of the scholarship committee, overcome significant
adversity in his or her quest for higher education.*

*The scholarship covers the full cost of tuition for
the academic year, and includes a stipend to defray the
expenses of housing, board, and materials. It is renew-
able each year, commensurate with satisfactory academic progress.*

*The enclosed information includes a more detailed
description of the scholarship, its provisions and requirements, as well as several forms for you to complete and
return. If you have any questions or need any further
information, please feel free to contact me.*

In the meantime, please accept my heartfelt con-
gratulations and best wishes for a promising academic
career.

Sincerely,
Edith J. Pearl
Dean of Admissions

38

He fills out forms. For everything he needs to do, there seems
to be a corresponding form. It began even before he completed
the landing card on the plane the day he arrived. It began with
a visa application. Then something called a relocation agreement. Then, early on, an application for the health insurance
that would eventually pay for his visits with Paul. Some of
these forms he completes with the assistance of a volunteer
from the Friends International Assistance Society, but quickly
his ability to fill them out by himself improves.

There is a residence card application, school admission
forms, class enrollment forms, host family questionnaires. Because he receives monetary support, there are tax forms,
academic progress reports, something called an "Adaptation
Report," which is used, he figures out, to determine his level of
social isolation.

Early on, he must complete a form to obtain a social security card. He is mildly surprised to find that it requests the same

information that is requested by the form he must complete to obtain a library card, and that they both request the same information as the form he must fill out for a video rental card.

To go to college he must take a standardized test, which he finds to be nothing more than a big, complicated form. Eventually, he will fill out forms to apply for college, then to enroll there, then to apply for an apartment near campus. He fills out more forms for school: emergency contact forms, allergy declarations, vaccination certificates, more insurance forms.

Curious about this peculiar obsession with filling out forms, he does some research in the library. (He does this research on the same day he fills out the form to apply for his library card.) He reads that over the course of a lifetime the average person living in America will spend six months filling out forms. He learns that forms really didn't catch on until the late eighteen hundreds, when the volume of activities people were doing— being born, dying, and getting married the top three—grew so great that the Victorian mind felt the overwhelming need to organize them scientifically. He learns that the form, in its current form, was originally called a formulary, and was invented by an Englishman named Charles Babbage, the same man who invented both an early kind of computer and the cow catcher, a device attached to the front of locomotives to clear debris from train tracks. He learns that Babbage once wrote to Alfred Tennyson to correct two lines from one of Tennyson's poems, which Babbage felt lacked scientific accuracy. This, thinks Jonas, tells you everything you need to know about both the man and the invention of forms.

He will fill out forms to apply for a credit card (he will be denied), to sign up for classes, once he is enrolled in the university, to obtain a bank account, into which his scholarship money is deposited, to reapply for a credit card (accepted this time, with a limit of five hundred dollars, which he will immediately spend on pizza, beer, and a series of baseball games).

Aptly named, the form, he feels. For not only is it orderly in appearance, but it also gives form to that which is hidden. His name, his age, ethnicity, religion, all mental constructs, made manifest through the use of forms. Collected passively, placed on blank lines waiting for answers, the information allows for the efficient counting, sorting, ordering, and categorizing of him, the actual thing the forms represent.

Filling out the forms helps Jonas memorize this information. The ink, usually black, as required by the form, sometimes blue, which Jonas prefers, flows from his pen and into the shapes of the letters and numbers that signify him. Often, after he completes a form, he has the eerie feeling of having just replicated himself, sending off a paper copy that will then live in the files of a cabinet in some warehouse, or be inputted into a computer. To the clerk at the bank or school or business or library or government agency, the form is now him. "Ah, yes," the form says to its reader, "I can tell you all you need to know." He feels dissected and displayed. Worse, he has begun to wonder what all these replicas of himself will get up to, once they are set free.

Nauseated by the thought of filling out yet another form, much less being tested for anything, he refuses to get a driver's license.

39

The first time he sees her, she is surrounded by a field of poppies.

It's their freshman year. They are at a Remembrance Sunday reception in the ornate English classroom in the Cathedral of Learning, to which he assumes they have been invited because of their connections to Commonwealth countries. The wood-paneled room, one of the towering, Gothic building's many nationality-themed classrooms, was built after the war with artifacts rescued from the bombed ruins of the House of Commons, then transported across the Atlantic to be presented to the university as a gift. Something about it, the smell, or the way the light falls on the thick-grained tables, reminds Jonas of his boyhood schoolroom, and he feels as though it had been built especially for him. Tonight it is filled with gray-haired men and women and a smattering of students, all of whom wear the red-paper flowers of remembrance. She is tall and willowy and dark and cuts through the pomp like a thorn. Like a rose.

He stands at the long table filled with hors d'oeuvres and bottled water, speaking with one of the English professors. He watches her peripherally, tracking her red dress and graceful legs. He reaches out to pick up some sort of crab cake or cream puff, stretching his arm out of the sleeve as he does so, and sees the professor to whom he is speaking notice the scar on his forearm. He pulls the sleeve down.

"Climbing a tree as a child," he says. "I fell."

Then, unexpectedly, they are standing next to each other, both of them sipping from their warm bottles of water, looking intently at stained-glass windows bearing the coats of arms of various famous English institutions or people. Her name tag says Shakri.

"India?" he says.

"Delhi," she says. "And you?"

Unlike him, he thinks, she wears her accent beautifully, effortlessly, like wings.

He tells her to guess, like he did, but she gives up after three tries.

Together they tour the room, closely regarding the oak desks, appraising two chairs rescued from Parliament and set in the place of honor at the head of the room, near the fireplace. "What do you want to bet they sat in someone's loo?" says Jonas. "There's an Englishman somewhere chuckling about that."

He tries desperately to think of something else clever to say, something to make her laugh again, but everything he can think of seems contrived or forced. He asks her whether she enjoyed the cream puffs, then silently curses his mouth for allowing such inanity to escape it.

In the end, Shakri herself provides the opening. She asks him, with a forwardness that catches him off guard, whether he doesn't want to just bag it and go for french fries—chips, she calls them—at the O, a local dive known for its french fries.

"Sure," he says, trying to force himself to sound relaxed.

They cross the broad lawn outside the cathedral in the dusky light. He experiences her as a presence walking beside him, a voice. He does not want to look directly at her for fear that he will end up simply staring. So he looks straight ahead as they talk about school, his friends, her family, movies and music, likes and dislikes, and anything else they can come up with, all the mundane details, all the minutiae of existence, but it is really just a pretext to be close to her, an excuse to extend their time, because all he can think is bliss.

40

Absent a nation, he creates his own. There is no initiation, no Pledge of Allegiance, no flag. Just a vague understanding, a discomfited sense of belonging. Hakma the Kurd is the first, and between the two of them, he and Jonas accrete new citizens, they joke, like a ball of tar.

They are different. They are slanty-eyed and dark-skinned. Their names are different. They are Ching Ji and Sinhal and Lhotsu and Thierry, the French kid they mostly just put up with because he pays for everything. They are Trevor from Zimbabwe, or from London, where he added a cockney twang to his southern African dialect of hollowed vowels and soft consonants (speaking, they tease him, like Nelson Mandela would speak if he found work as a chimney sweep). They are James, from Montana, who is someone's roommate and who, as he is frequently reminded, is kept around as the token Yankee, a trapping of respectability, to be traded or sold at any convenient moment. They are interestingly garbed, avant-garde, and nerdy. They listen to diverse music: electronica and funk, jazz and reggae. One of them may be royalty.

They are known everywhere, whether they are welcomed at chic lounges by bartenders who are eager to add a touch of ethnicity to their ambience, or they are the dark kids in the corner, most likely engineering students, who talk funny. Or maybe they are something in between, something more like their classmates, like everyone of a certain age: on their own, confident and self-absorbed and accomplished and immature and cruel and generous and smart and unconcerned and cavalier and sensitive and ambitious, and, and, and.

41

This sticks in my mind.

They tell us to put on our gas masks. They file us into a low, cinder-block hut. They make us stand against the walls. The sergeant enters and closes the door behind him. In the middle of the room is a low, wrought-iron table, and on top of it sits a silver cylinder, like a thermos. Its edges are brown with liquid stains, like coffee. The sergeant twists off the top of the cylinder and drops in several white pellets, releasing a thin haze. Then we are all ordered to take off our masks. None of us wants to do it. But he is yelling at us, telling us we will be court-martialed if we don't.

My eyes tear up as soon as I take off the mask, and I gag on the smoke entering my lungs. We all start coughing up thick gobs of mucus, and our skin burns like it's under a heat lamp. I

panic, nearly dropping the mask. I think I can see the silhouettes
of people burned onto the walls. Just when I think I am going to
black out, he tells us to put our masks back on. My skin still burns,
but with the mask on, at least I can see clearly and breathe. After
a minute, we are ordered to take off our masks again. This time
we do it quickly, knowing that the faster we get them off, the faster
we will be allowed to get them back on. This done, we file quickly
out of the building and fall into a retching mass on the cool grass
outside.

42

He soon finds that, except to those in the middle of it, being
in love is the most boring thing, the most incomprehensible
thing in the world.

They dine at a secluded corner table on a red-and-white
paper tablecloth, upon which the food before them either loses
all meaning or becomes their entire existence. Her hands fly
around as she talks, seeming to push the words through the air
in front of her, and he hangs from them like a strand of over-
cooked fettuccini.

She tells him that, were the earth the size of an apple, the
surface would be as smooth as its skin. This bit of trivia feels
vitally important to him, as though it says something funda-
mental about their lives. He finds it amusing when she tries to
show him the correct way to hold a fork. He tells her that if
you hold your hand at arm's length out to the night sky, an area

of the night equivalent to the space of your thumbnail would contain a million stars, most of which cannot even be seen by the naked eye. By which he means that present between them are infinite possibilities.

And they are only dimly aware that, to an outside observer, someone lacking their interest or enthusiasm or imagination, they are talking a kind of silly code, a special language known only to them.

43

Paul has read an article, and is struck by the coincidence.

Jonas does not want to talk about it.

He was called Christopher.

"That's amazing, don't you think?" says Paul.

Jonas says nothing.

They know only that he was involved. He was called Christopher. And now Paul has read a story in the newspaper. He was from a town not too far away. His mother still lives there.

Jonas looks out the window.

They know he went off to war and that he did not come back. He did not, as they say, make it. But he was there, and he was involved, and maybe, just maybe, says Paul, that is something.

44

The first time Shakri asks him up to her apartment, it is all he can do to keep from bounding up the stairs ahead of her. They have been seeing each other for more than a month, and her sudden forwardness surprises him.

They kiss as she searches for her keys, kiss as she opens the door, kiss as she does not turn on the light. It is as though she has made up her mind. They fumble around over their clothes, awkwardly at first, as though learning the intricacies of sign language, but then with increased fluency, and then one of them suddenly learns how to undo a button, and it is all down-hill from there.

45

Occasionally he is asked: Why America?

Sometimes he gives the long answer. Sometimes he says the question asks him, he feels, a larger question, asks him to place his experience in a global context. Secretly he enjoys this, likes being thought of as part of a movement, although he would never openly admit to this. Instead, he says that he had nothing, and that they came to him and offered him a choice.

Sometimes he mentions the Pakistanis and Indians living

generations deep in Bradford and Manchester, or the Congolese in Brussels, or Algerians and Moroccans in Paris, or Vietnamese throughout California. He has read about them, studied them in school, and even though he feels more alone than he imagines any of these other people must feel, secure as they are in their mobile communities, he tries to place his experience into the frame of these movements, into the complex relationship between victor and vanquished, colonizer and colonized.

A *diaspora.* A sociology professor first used that word to describe him, and he likes it, although he is careful not to reveal the satisfaction he derives from it. He practices using the word casually, in conversation. Diaspora. "As a member of the global diaspora, I feel . . ." And then he is off, propelled by the authority of membership. He likes how it sounds, but mostly he likes the word because of its hints of mystery and power, its implication of choice, all of which are entirely removed when the word "refugee" is used.

Sometimes, though, he doesn't give the long answer. Sometimes he gives the short one. Why America? Because he had a choice. The same choice we always have. Stay or go.

And, given the choice, he went.

46

But the thing is, in all that time, I don't really remember making a decision. I don't remember saying to myself, "Yes, I will do this," or,

"No, I will not do that." They tell you what to do, and you do it. You don't reflect on it. You don't ponder its meaning. You don't explore its ambiguities or consider its consequences. These burdens are removed from you. In theory, these burdens are removed from you.

But you are still human. Eventually, you do reflect on it. The consequences make themselves known. The results of your actions persist. Eventually, you are struck by their meaning. At some point, an accounting is made. Eventually, if you are human, and sane, you examine what you have done.

47

Together, Jonas and Shakri go to movies, to clubs, to parties at the homes of friends and acquaintances. They are seen walking hand in hand across the cathedral lawn after dinner. In public, they are reserved, formal, but they devour each other with their glances. Sinhal claims to have seen them kissing, but is thought to be exaggerating. Trevor catches them on a late Saturday morning at Bart's Café, sitting in the low lounge chairs set around vast coffee tables. Shakri drinks hot chocolate and Jonas tea, while they both read newspapers.

"You two's already like an old married couple," says Trevor as he sits down, forcing himself between them, cheeky and smiling and pulling an earphone out of his ear. "Sitting reading your papers. Me, I don't want a married life till well after thirty!"

Jonas and Shakri look up from their reading.

"We're not married, man," says Jonas.

"Get your feet off the table, Trevor," says Shakri.

48

Paul has read an article about Christopher, but Jonas does not want to hear about it. During a session Paul mentions it, and Jonas does not respond.

The next session, Paul brings it up again. Christopher's mother is called Rose. Rose Henderson. Jonas is not interested. He says only that he is comfortable not knowing, but in reality he feels his stomach tighten each time Paul mentions it.

"You have to admit, it's quite a coincidence," says Paul.

The next session, Paul has brought the newspaper article, which he hands to Jonas like a summons. Jonas doesn't want to look, doesn't want to know, but sees no way to get out of it.

The article takes up most of an inside page, its only illustration being a black-and-white sketch of Rose Henderson. Despite himself, Jonas is transfixed. When he is finished reading it, he reads it again. And when he has read it for the fourth time, he looks up at Paul and says, "Could this . . . I mean, is it possible?" And then he sits silently, looking down at the newspaper in his lap.

Eventually, Paul says, "Would you like to go and talk with her?"

49

Shakri is by far the more dedicated student, planning to follow her family's expected path and go to medical school. She studies for hours at a stretch, biology and chemistry, and a measure of her dedication seems to wear off onto Jonas, who to this point has gotten through school by, as he puts it, "brains and bullshit."

"I go to class," he says, his voice almost a whine. "Do that and you barely have to read anything! We were doing *The Odyssey*, and I only read the last three chapters. Wouldn't you know it; the final exam was just one question: 'Analyze the major themes of *The Odyssey*, referencing only three chapters.' The professor called it the best essay she ever read on the subject."

"She mustn't have read many."

50

On a Saturday afternoon Shakri and Jonas sit in low, open lounge chairs at Bart's. Shakri drinks hot chocolate, which she loves, going through two or three tublike cups of it a day, even in the summer.

Jonas drinks tea. He has kept only a few connections to

the past, and this is one of them. He likes it sweet and strong, and if it is just the right kind—spiced kava, served with a hard sweet the way they do at Bart's—then even the smell of it is comforting. He usually has at least a cup of it a day, more if he drank too much the night before. It's one o'clock, and he's on his fifth cup.

It's a pretty day, autumn and cold, and the sun streams in through the window and highlights Shakri's dark skin and eyes and hair, and Jonas thinks to himself that she really is striking, and he also thinks that maybe he should tell her this. And then he thinks that maybe he shouldn't. He doesn't want to mess anything up by drawing attention to it, does not want to appear fawning or overly demonstrative, refrains from outwardly valuing anything he fears may be taken away. He prefers to appreciate things from a distance.

And then finally he opens his mouth and says: "I was so trashed last night."

"I know," says Shakri, and Jonas avoids her glare by looking studiously out the window. "You passed out cold on my couch. I woke up and you were gone."

He doesn't seem to remember all of this, although he does vaguely remember seeing her, and being surprised to find himself on her sofa with the sun streaming through the window, and then walking home in the early light, not wanting to wake her. The rest of the night, though, is a blur. But there is a detail, an image from the night before that he does remember, that stands out in his mind, and he tells this to Shakri, explains it to her. Then he tells her that you have a choice about how you react to things.

They sit for a while longer in their silence. Jonas is not too distressed by the hangover, and in fact he takes a certain pleasure in the distance it gives him from reality, the tingling fingers, the vague light-headedness, which somehow seems to heighten his other senses. He is fascinated by the intricate dance of waiters to and from the kitchen, the busy clink of plates and glasses in his good left ear, the sunlight falling through the large window and into his sparkling teacup, the hum of conversation and New Agey music. For just a second he thinks that he might be able to hear something out of his right ear, high and distant, like someone whistling, or birds singing on the wind.

"Jonas!" says Shakri, and it is apparent from her tone that this is the second or possibly third time she has called to him.

"Sorry," he says, turning to meet her eyes.

"Over here, man," she says, snapping her fingers up next to her head. "What did Paul say yesterday?"

Jonas thinks back to his session the previous afternoon, which seems a very long time ago. "He said my mental health is surprisingly good."

"He always says that."

"He said I might want to consider not drinking for a while."

"Uh-huh."

"He said I might think about going to see her, this lady, this soldier's mother, thinks it might help me fit things together," he says, realizing even as he does so that to say it out loud is to give shape to something he had wanted to remain formless.

"And what do you think?"

They sit there for a moment, Shakri looking at him expectantly, and then he is certain that in the middle of their silence he can hear something in his deaf right ear, some kind of signal coming through, like strings faintly plucked.

"He said it might give me a sense of closure."

"So you'll do it?"

"I don't know. Maybe."

"I'll drive you, if you want."

"Maybe," he says.

"You should do it."

"I don't know."

The noise fades in and out, the soft, high song, and he turns to look out the windows, convinced he'll see some mysterious musician strumming a sitar, but there is only the street, filled with afternoon light and bustling pedestrians.

51

It was supposed to have been a mellow evening.

Hakma, Trevor, and Jonas take the crosstown bus to listen to jazz on the South Side. They are going to relax. They meet up with a few other people, acquaintances more than friends, who seem to converge every time they go out. Mike, or maybe Mark, from Philadelphia. Luca, who just broke up with his girl-friend. The weekend unfurls like so many weekends among people who might be known to one another by a first name and a single personal detail, these details providing the basis for an evening's lurching conversation, more fluid as the night and the drinks carry on, forgotten by morning until the next weekend, or maybe the next, when the same conversation rolls around again, fresh.

The jazz is modern stuff, which is usually not really Jonas's thing, but the trumpeter is particularly good, playing high and wailing off the piano's depth in unexpected ways, here a mass of unrelated notes, there a perfectly balanced chord progression, unexpected, discordant when they expect harmony, harmonious when they least expect that, alternately keeping them on edge, then lulling them.

They drink. By the end of the set they are convinced that they have just witnessed the future of musical expression: subversive, glorious, embodying all to which music should aspire.

When it ends they cross the street to the Astrid, their conversation loud and animated, and as usual Hakma is talking about Kurdistan. The incarnation of injustice, what the Turks do to us, he says. You just don't understand. Has he ever been there, someone asks, one of the stragglers, obviously, someone who does not yet know this question's inadvisability until he asks it. Yes, says Hakma, and his parents were born there, and his parents' parents, and their blood is his blood, and almost everyone, except for the person who asked the ill-advised question, starts to pay attention to other things, because this is the conversation they have every week, fueled by injustice and rounds of drinks.

The room starts to whirl ever so slightly from the edges, left to right, and Jonas focuses on a knot on the wooden tabletop, only to watch it move slowly to the right, along with the rest of the room, and he has to move his eyes to keep up with it, but he can't get the timing right and his eyes slip past the knot, then move back to try to focus on it again.

Of course *you* understand me, Hakma is saying; *you* are my brothers, my sisters, my comrades against evil, my long-odds risk takers, my fellow freedom fighters. He is really going for it, trying to impress the inapt questioner with the nobility of his plight. Jonas remains silent for much of this conversation. Hakma looks over at him occasionally; they all do, as though looking for permission, or affirmation. Jonas has never spoken directly of his childhood to any of them, but people hear things, divine things from what is left unsaid, and it is widely believed that he holds the trump card in the suit of injustice.

Across the table, Hakma grows louder. They don't get it. Nobody gets it. He raises his voice to a level that seems very loud, but for all anyone knows may simply be appropriate. They have no idea what his people have suffered, goddamned Turks, and he no longer looks around to see whether any of *them* might be present. The uselessness of NATO, and Europe, and America, America the cowardly, America the impotent. They don't know, can't know, can't understand. And then someone comes over, someone big, with a backward baseball cap and very white gym shoes, comes over and tells him to be quiet, to shut the fuck up, and there's some shoving, and the room spins again, and then they're grabbing their coats, and they're hustled out into the yellow-lit street.

Someone has the idea to go to another bar. A better bar. A cooler bar. This bar is loungier, big chairs, low tables, and Jonas sees that the trumpet player they saw earlier is at this bar, and it's a small neighborhood, so he's not really surprised to see him there, tall and skinny and wearing a captain's cap, and his music is playing over the sound system, the same music they had all just heard, but perhaps because of this it strikes them as a thin echo of what they heard live. He knows the bartender, this musician, and they are in the midst of an animated conversation about the music, both of them bopping their heads in time to it.

They all sit down and order beer and resume the conversation, injustice and power, but like the music, it is all getting old for Jonas, thin, and before long he says he's going home. What he really wants to do is go back to Shakri, collapse into her. He gets up and puts on his jacket. Hakma grows quiet. They all shake hands and exchange loose hugs. Trevor drifts off with another friend, and Hakma is left at the table by himself.

Jonas turns around to leave, pulls his coat collar up around his neck. The door opens and he rides out into the cool street on a current of warm air and plaintive trumpet. Once he's outside, he looks back in through the bar's big picture window, and sees the image he will tell Shakri about the next day, while he sits with her sipping tea.

The bar's canned light spills out through the window and onto the street, so it's a little like looking at a giant TV screen. The left side of the bar is awash with people milling about, talking, a series of animated heads and dark clothes, laughing, carrying drinks. On the right side of the barroom is a low table at which Hakma sits alone, lit from above as if by a gentle spotlight, his half-finished beer on the table in front of him, his arms resting on his knees, fingers together, interlaced, his head bowed as if in prayer.

52

Tuesday, September 25 (AP)—Johnstown, Pennsylvania, resident Rose Henderson has only questions, and she wants only answers.

"At first, when they told me he was lost, I thought they just meant lost as in misplaced, like maybe he caught the wrong plane somewhere and he would turn up eventually," she says, referring to her son Christopher, who went missing in action while serving with the Seventh Cavalry Regiment. She speaks with the practiced weariness of someone who has repeated a story many times. "Then, a few weeks later, I got this very official-looking letter that said he had been formally declared missing in action. But they wouldn't say where he was, or how it happened, or why.

"Eventually, we learned a few more things about it," she said recently over a cup of tea in her living room, which has been turned into something of a shrine to her eldest son. A large portrait of him hangs over the mantelpiece, and commendation letters, school trophies, and snapshots are displayed on shelves in a bookcase.

Years later, she says the worst part is not knowing for sure, not having closure. "We were going to hold a memorial service a few years ago, but it just seemed wrong. If there's even a chance he's still alive, however small . . ." At this, Rose's voice trails off, before she is able to take in a breath and continue. "At the same time, I wish there were some kind of end to this."

A spokesman from the Department of Defense, Richard Dominick, refused to discuss the specifics of the case.

In an effort to get more information, she repeatedly contacted her congressional representatives. When she still didn't hear anything, she formed a support group of other military families, many of whom have suffered lost, injured, or killed family members.

"At first it was small, just local. We have a lot of families in the service around here. But pretty soon we were being contacted by people from all over."

The support group, which numbers over one hundred families, calls itself Military Families for Truth. And while they haven't been able to get all the information they believe is available about the loss of Christopher, they have been able to help the families of other soldiers.

"Many of them were misclassified," says Henderson. "Or there was some kind of other clerical error. We're pretty good at getting them to go back and make sure they have told us everything they can, and often, when they look at it again, they realize they can tell us more than they have."

She says that helping other families deal with the loss of their loved ones has helped her deal with her own loss. "He was my first-born son," says Henderson, who is divorced from Christopher's father, and has two younger children who are now grown and live away from home. "The group has brought me up a little," she says. "I was depressed for such a long time, and it helps to know that there are others in similar situations, and that I can help them."

In the meantime, Rose Henderson is still looking for answers. "I don't know if I'll ever learn the whole truth," she says. "But I've got to keep looking."

53

It gets in there, this thought, this way of thinking. They try to plant it, for sure, tend to it so that it grows, foster it, but it is in there to begin with. You're born with it, I suppose, and eventually life takes it out of you. The notion that you're invincible. No fear, they said. They don't want you to have any fear. Those other things, that invincibility, that aggression. They bring it out in you, show you how to do things, try to teach you how not to be stupid, how to protect each other. Protect each other. Be aggressive. Protect each other.

And then one day you find out what that really means.

54

If he has one complaint about Shakri, it is her tendency, in his view, occasionally, not always, but sometimes, to dominate him. At first, he finds it comforting, like a blanket or an old pair of jeans, and he submits himself to it willingly, even eagerly. It shows she cares about him.

She buys him a new shirt as a present, requesting that he wear it out that evening. She has a car, and insists on driving him everywhere—to class, to the store, to the park, to his friends' apartments—even when he wants to walk. He suspects she wants to make sure he is where he says he is.

She says the sight of a cheeseburger makes her physically ill, asks him not to order it, then buys him dietary supplements the next day to compensate for the lost protein. She asks where they are going, purses her lips disapprovingly at his answer, and drives them someplace else.

She talks to him at length about his diet, particularly his drinking, his clothes, his study habits. Once, he comes to see her smelling of cigarette smoke, and she stands over him, hands flying wildly, talking for nearly an hour about cancer, while he tries in vain to tell her it was Trevor who was smoking.

55

The road to Johnstown is built from slabs of grooved cement, laid end-to-end with a small gap between them to accommodate the winter cycle of freezing and thawing. Subsidence tilts the slabs gently away from one another, and driving on the road is like driving over an endless series of roughly laid patios. As usual when he rides in a car, the motion nauseates Jonas, and he diligently regards the scenery to prevent himself from getting sick. The previous winter's black cinders line the road, and a multitude of auto-body shops careen past as they drive, as does the brilliant red-and-yellow foliage of autumn.

"Can you believe we ended up here?" asks Shakri, her accent fluttering in a way that seems to imply she is talking more about herself than about Jonas. He shrugs. Snow flurried across the hills a few days before, but today is unseasonably warm, and he opens his window partway to let in some fresh air.

"I didn't know this was a possibility," he says.

"Could you put your window up?" she says. "I'm cold."

They drive past strip malls and cornfields, churches and forests, low one-floor houses with long, straight driveways and properties well delineated from the surrounding tangle of overgrowth merely by the fact of being mowed, all of it a revelry in the American urge toward expansion. There do not seem to be towns or cities in the usual senses of those words, but only certain areas where there are more buildings and certain areas where there are fewer. Each family has staked out a large section of ground, built a house in the middle of it, and those sections string together, stretching from one built-up area to another, filling up everything, as though everyone everywhere is spreading out their arms in a vast display of ownership.

The hills steepen as they drive closer to Johnstown, and the trees have lost almost all of their leaves at the higher elevation. Piles of snow appear beside the road, which clacks along underneath them like a train track. The houses, white and pink and gray clapboard, crowd the hillside, along with the melting remnants of the unusually early snowfall. Jonas pulls from his pocket a slip of paper with Rose's address and directions scrawled on it, and they exit the highway.

The neighborhood is large, full of large houses set back from the oak-lined streets, large lawns better cared-for than those at the majority of houses they have passed, and large cars sitting in the driveways. Shakri slows the car as they search the mailboxes on the odd-numbered side of the street for number forty-five.

The house sits on a small rise, and it looks perhaps taller than the earth-and-timber houses Jonas remembers from his youth, but of about the same overall area. A massive oak crowds the front yard, and from beside the front door a picture window looks out on the well-kept lawn. Jonas gets out of the car and is struck by how much cooler it is here than in the city.

His heart doesn't start beating quickly until he is walking up to the front door, past the carefully tended shrubs and a light in the front yard made to look like an old-fashioned street lamp. Shakri follows along behind, for once waiting as he makes the first move. He thinks about turning around, getting back in the car, and having her drive him home. But she is a presence behind him, and he realizes that the odds of convincing her to leave are remote. Then he sees the curtain in the large window move, and knows that he has been seen. He walks up to the door, takes a deep breath, and rings the bell.

56

He hears Rose's voice almost before he sees her, the door swinging open and there she is, a tiny woman with a flash of red hair and blue eyes and a sort of sideways smile, not forced, but perhaps strained.

"You must be Jonas," she says, and when he hears her voice he is slightly stunned, both by its volume—such a large sound from such a small person—but also because it is as if he is hearing the original voice for the first time, the accent stronger, a distant echo of the voice he heard long before, high up on a mountain.

"Yes," he says, "Jonas," pitching his own voice almost unnaturally lower, as though doing so will somehow force Rose to adopt a quieter tone, an effort which seems to have the opposite effect.

"Such a nice name!" she booms across the neighborhood, and then she steps out onto the porch and hugs him awkwardly, during which time his arms hang, useless and pinned to his body by her embrace. "And who's this?"

"This is Shakri," he says, watching as Shakri extends her arm to shake hands, only to go wide-eyed and limp during another long embrace.

"Well, that's a pretty name, too!" says Rose, stepping back to look her over. "Fits such a pretty girl. Well, why don'tcha come on in." And she steps aside to let them into the house.

The house is as well cared for inside as the yard is outside, with dark, polished furniture and cream carpets and a tall, ornate grandfather clock in the corner, all of it lit by soft sunlight diffused through thin muslin curtains. The windows are open to the gentle breeze, and when he walks into the living room, Jonas catches his breath.

Over the fireplace is a portrait that dominates the room, nearly the size of the fireplace itself. It *is* him. The face is so familiar but also different, younger and less worn than he remembers it. The crow's-feet have not yet developed around his eyes, and the hair is freshly shorn. He wears a dress blue uniform, and the American flag behind him is so crisp that Jonas can almost see it waving in the cool breeze that puffs in through the open windows. The face looks out at them from its place over the mantel as though presiding over a court.

"Can I get you something to drink?" asks Rose, already on her way to the kitchen to retrieve it. "Water or pop or something?"

"Just some water," says Shakri, but Jonas doesn't say anything. He can't take his eyes off the picture over the mantel. In it, Christopher looks as though he has just graduated from school, maybe in his late teens. It is him, but it's not him at the same time, not Jonas's version of him. It's not the way he remembers him. It's a memory of him, but only one facet, the reality of the picture forcing itself onto everyone's perception, the way it dominates the room. This is not him, Jonas wants to say.

He can't stop looking at it.

When Rose comes back from the kitchen, she carries a plate of cookies and two tall glasses of juice, which she sets down on the coffee table, her hands trembling ever so slightly. Jonas notices that she also has something else. Tucked under her arm is a thick manila envelope.

"When your counselor called to tell me you were coming," she says, "I made this up to give to you." She holds the packet toward him, almost reluctantly. "I don't like to read them anymore, or look at the photos, but they might mean something to you."

Jonas takes the envelope from her and opens it, begins to

look through it, sees that it is full of photocopied press clippings and photographs, but Rose stops him, pushing it closed in his hands. "I'd prefer if you would look at it somewhere else," she says, and she is gentle about it, but firm, so he closes the packet and tucks it under his arm.

At some point Rose notices that Jonas keeps glancing at the portrait over the mantel.

"I practically begged him not to go," she says. "As a mother, you're not supposed to say this, but as soon as he told me, I knew he wasn't coming back." Jonas senses a certain comfort she takes in telling them this, in thinking of it all as preordained. "But that's the way things work out sometimes. Everything happens for a reason. Don't you think so, Jonas?"

They're sitting down now, he and Shakri on the sofa and Rose in a chair across from them, a glass-topped table between.

"I don't know," he says, hesitating as he reluctantly turns his attention away from the picture. "Sometimes I do."

Rose smiles, and it's the most subtle gesture she has made since they arrived. "Tell me," she says, "your counselor, what's his name?"

"Paul."

"Right, Paul. He didn't really give me a lot of detail. I'm— he may have told you—I'm always looking for information. The military is often not too forthcoming."

Jonas is staring at the portrait again, but now he sees that Rose notices, that she recognizes how intently he looks at it, at him, at the portrait of her son, and there is a flash of recognition. She rounds on Jonas, focused. And then she seems to catch herself; not wanting to spook him, easily as she can, she says, gently but firmly, as though handling shards of glass, "Tell me, Jonas"—her voice catches in her throat—"did you know my Christopher?"

The room is bathed in a diffuse glow, the early-afternoon breeze, the grandfather clock ticking away in the corner. Rose's face has been forced into a mask, fixed in place by an end-less cycle of yearning and disappointment, a calm exterior laid over a mix of curiosity and something else. Hope.

Jonas hesitates. His mind is a whirl of images and half-remembered events, and he is aware mostly of the necessity of choosing his words carefully, of the importance of the next few moments, of the unbearable weight of both lies and truth. He gathers together his will. Once he begins, he unwinds a story that is, like all stories, a mix of memory and impression. But he does his best to be mindful of his audience, to make it a sensi-tive story, an appropriate story, and for the hour he takes to tell it, his voice never quavers once.

"Your son saved my life," begins Jonas. And that, at least in part, is the truth.

REMEMBRANCE

Something had happened. Something awful.

He remembers the cool night air flowing in through the open window, the thin woolen blanket keeping the warmth close to his body. He was young enough that he still shared a room with his sister, Miriam. But she was not there. Something had happened.

He remembers armed men running down the street in front of the house, and his mother wailing. He had been sent to bed early, told to stay there. And from his pallet on the floor he listened to low voices, his father and brother, occasional shouts in the street, the arrivals and departures of visitors.

He must have fallen asleep, and it was quiet when he woke. The cool night air flowed in through the open window, carrying with it the strangely bright light from a crescent moon. Under the woolen blanket, Younis turned on his side, trying to get comfortable.

He remembers thinking that the next year, or perhaps the year after, when his brother had moved out to start his own family, he would sleep in his own room, now his brother's room, toward the front of the house. But for now he shared a room, a children's room, with his sister, who was not there. Their soft rugs lay against opposite walls, and he felt the cool autumn air streaming in through the window, even as the blanket held close his warmth.

His body warm, his face pleasantly cool, he smelled the faint, lingering scent of woodsmoke high on the air, and then he became aware of an increasingly urgent pressure on his bladder. At first he tried to deny it, and for a moment he contemplated rolling over, pulling the blanket around him, and trying to go back to sleep. Somewhere in the distance a rooster cleared its throat. He wanted to stay in bed, go back to sleep, because he knew that if he got out of bed and into the cold, sleep would have even more difficulty overtaking him when he returned. But then he found the urge was too great to ignore. He braced himself, then pulled back the blanket and allowed the cool air to envelop him, raising gooseflesh on his arms.

He stood up and tugged on his shalwar and kamiz. In the moonlight, he spotted his long, woolen wrap lying in a bundle against the wall, and thought about pulling it over his shoulders for warmth, then reconsidered. He would be gone only minutes, after all, because he was paying only a brief visit to the low earthen hut in the backyard. He strapped on his sandals and walked groggily out through the kitchen, opening the heavy wooden back door as silently as he could manage.

Dew covered the yard's cool grass, and wet his feet as he

crossed, taking practiced steps toward the small outbuilding at the far end of the wall. It was a clear night, with a thin sliver of moon low in the sky, and off to the east the horizon showed the first faint signs of the coming dawn. He wished absently that he weren't so tired, so that he might linger, appreciate it all awhile longer. He entered the outhouse, of habit holding his breath against the acrid smell, pulled the kamiz down slightly, and released his bladder. The rooster crowed again in the distance, and Younis was nearly finished when he heard the noise.

It cut sharply through the clear night, louder and louder. He will never be able to describe it adequately. It sounded like a lot of things: like paper ripping, amplified a hundred times, and overlaying that was the sound of a flag cracking rapidly in a strong wind, and some kind of engine noise, like a scooter with a broken tailpipe, and underneath it all was a low, long whistle, sounding for all the world like the whistle his father made when he called the sheep in from the far pasture. The entire cacophony grew louder and louder, but at the same time, in his memory, extended on until forever.

And then, at the far end of forever was an explosion. But to simply call it an explosion would be like calling the sun a light: literally true but grossly insufficient. It was the crossing of a barrier, a rending of reality. It was light brighter than he had ever seen, and then he was blind; it was louder than imagination, and then he was deaf. He was slammed against the back wall of the outhouse, and then there was nothing.

2

He woke to shouts and more explosions, kept distant by a ringing sound in his right ear. He was still in the outhouse, the walls of which jumped with shadows cast by nearby firelight, distorted flickers on the wall. He got to his knees and peered out, trying to stretch his arm to support himself, but was stopped short by a stab of pain from his wrist to his shoulder. It felt as though his arm were slowly being torn in two. He clutched at his arm to find that it was wet, and this confused him. He curled the arm to his stomach and pushed himself up to kneel on the earthen floor. He stood weakly and looked down to see large wet patches covering the front of his clothes. His sleeve was ripped almost from the wrist to the elbow, and he moved his arm tentatively, stopping when pain ran up to his shoulder and into his chest. He stumbled out of the outbuilding.

The crescent moon still hung over the horizon, and the eastern sky was not much brighter than it was the last time he looked at it, but everything else was different. His house was gone, in its place a pile of broken stone and burning timbers, the air filled with the charred, pungent smell of smoldering plastic. Flames roared through empty windows in the shattered wall. He considered running back in, took a step forward, then another, but with each step the heat grew exponentially, burning his skin and drying his eyes, until he was barely able even to look at it. He realized he was yelling.

More explosions burst forth from other parts of the village, each preceded by the same nameless sound, and it seemed as though nothing existed in the world except explosions. Younis found himself wondering whether every one of them meant the same thing.

He briefly thought he might be asleep still, in his bed and dreaming it all. The explosions stopped, replaced now by shouts and wails. A diffuse firelight rose and fell all around him, rose and fell, illuminating towering columns of thick black smoke hulking above all the world, fading into the darkness, return-ing again, massive and dangerous, like monsters disappearing and reappearing from the corners of his bedroom.

Younis moved through it all in a state of hyperawareness, not thinking in the rational sense, but rapidly processing pieces of information, noticing, slowing everything down. He noticed how a small part of the house's back wall, the part farthest away from the outhouse, looked normal, completely unaffected by the carnage around it. He smelled the acrid smell of burning plastic and hair and the sulfur smell of explosives. He noticed that the water well in the courtyard appeared to be untouched, the circular retaining wall pristine, but that something sat on it in flames, as though someone had balanced a burning leg of mutton on the well's lip. Tiny craters pocked the outhouse's mud-brick outer walls, and the courtyard wall buckled in upon itself.

He still held his arm curled up at his stomach, and he

looked down to see that blood dripped off the tips of his fingers
and into the dewy grass. He wrapped his forearm in a loose
piece of his shalwar, keeping his elbow bent, the fabric wound
tightly.

He felt himself go weak, and fought to maintain consciousness. For a moment, he thought he might be able to fly,
lift himself off the ground and swoop away toward the hills,
where he knew his family awaited him, willing his speedy
journey.

The first gunshots came from the south side of the village,
sharp, small reports, one or two at a time, like the sound of
kindling under an ax. Then a machine gun opened up and the
pops came as rapidly as the chain links through the pulley over
the well when the bucket was dropped in, the whole chaos of
reports moving gradually closer.

Younis ran toward the front gate, which led out onto the
street, noticing when he got there that the entire wall beside
the gate was now one long pile of bricks that he could have
easily stepped over. Despite this, he popped open the latch
and let the heavy door swing wide, closing it firmly after he
exited.

The street itself was deserted, but he heard the mass of
gunfire and shouts moving toward him like a living thing,
faster and faster, louder by the second. He turned to go in the
opposite direction, and took a single step when suddenly the
world opened up all around, the gate and remnants of the wall
behind him bursting into chips and splinters and showering
him with dust.

The shouts came from everywhere at once, up the street and down, the air around him filling with cracks and whistles. He wanted to lie down, become the earth. He wanted to wake himself up, surround himself with iron and stone, drift away like dust before a windstorm. Instead, he spotted the narrow alleyway between two houses opposite the pile of rubble that used to be his home. He ran across the street and down the alley, the walls barely wide enough for his shoulders to pass through, and into another alley, and then another, all of them familiar and yet completely foreign. And then he was on the road beside the river, the broad expanse of water dark against the growing dawn.

Gunfire echoed again somewhere behind him, but he stopped despite it, suddenly stunned by the river. He probably looked at it for no more than a second or two, but the moment stretches on in his memory, expanding and becoming an event all its own. He was taken in by the beauty of it, by its cold rapids still roiling away, unconcerned by the horror unfolding behind him. For a moment he took in the sound of it, the gentle gurgle closer to shore, a top note underpinned by the deeper, more powerful roar out toward the rushing center. It will never stop, he thought, flowing on and building as it headed south, emptying, finally, into the vast sea, taking with it the water at which he now gazed, as much that night's witness as himself, and yet fallow by comparison, unplanted with its brutality.

He considered jumping into it, letting the rushing water carry him along, whether to safety or not, where he would be silent and invisible in the churning current. He recalled swimming in it during the heat of summer, at the deep pool upstream, the icicles that shot through him when he jumped in from the rocky bank, numbing his legs and arms, bringing his life to the top of his skin, and he realized that in that water, those rapids, he would never survive the journey. And then he wondered whether he wanted to survive, and thought that maybe jumping in would be the best thing after all.

This happened much faster than it takes to describe, only seconds, and later Younis will express his amazement at this, at how quickly everything changes, whether because of a decision you make or the decisions made by others, or just because of chance, and in a moment the entire path of your life, everything you knew and everything you will ever know, is altered. But in those few seconds all he recognized was the need to make a decision and, somewhere deep inside, the importance of his choice.

The gunfire grew louder until it was nearly upon him, and he discovered he was running, only distantly aware of having decided to run, more conscious of the cool morning air blowing his hair, the rush of wind that he was puzzled to find he could hear only in his left ear, and he ran without knowing it, north out of the village, along the river, his legs churning without thought, like the river itself, and he ran down the path toward the hills, toward the mountains, running under the beautiful clear moon, toward the pass, and he ran, unconnected to the world, understanding nothing save the need to run, and he ran, and he was distantly surprised to find, almost offhandedly, that he did not cry, not even a tear.

3

Jonas pauses occasionally, to take a breath, or a sip from his glass of juice, or to gather his thoughts, and when he does, a little gap opens up in the space of the living room. Within these gaps live perceptions rendered undetectable by the telling of the story: the steady ticking of the grandfather clock in the corner, the creak of Rose's wooden chair as she shifts her weight, the echoed shout of a child playing out in the neighborhood, the lengthening shadows in the front yard.

Rose has heard stories like this before. Not this story, of course. This story is different. Each story is different. But all of them share a need to be told, to be heard, and Rose knows how to hear them. She knows that these gaps are important, that they mean something. She knows that often the gaps are nearly as important as the story itself.

And so, despite her growing apprehension, she does not try to fill them. She does not express astonishment, or make meaningless, encouraging sounds. She does not ask questions, does not request clarification. She listens. She gives him her attention, the space to find his words, allows his story to breathe, offers him this measure of grace.

The cave his father had described came to mean more in You-nis's mind than it actually was. He searched for hours, trying to match his father's instructions to the unfamiliar terrain before him, increasingly tired, weakened by the loss of blood, exhausted, and, finally, desperate. He longed for the cave, longed for all it represented. Its capacity for solace, its ability to shelter grew larger and more mythical with each step he took. He wandered across the empty hills.

Near the rock his father had shown him, balanced unnat-urally in the shallow water close to the bank, the path ran away from the river and wove past a low, rocky outcrop before ascending steeply. Into the hills, it leveled out as often as the terrain allowed, but mostly it climbed steeply. The route was clear close to the river, a visible footpath that he easily fol-lowed up into the low pastures. But farther into the hills, it traversed stone and gravel, so that he had to search every twenty or thirty steps to be sure he was still walking in the right direction.

Periodically, the route appeared to end abruptly, run straight into a rock wall or stand of brush. He scrambled up the stone face or around the brush, searching above it until he found the barest trace on which to continue, until the trail disappeared again, this time into a deep gully, or a stretch of impenetrable thorns, and he repeated the process, each time hoping that the path on which he resumed his trek was the correct one.

His route trended steeply upward, switching back and forth as it encountered obstacles and sheer faces, sometimes leading right back toward the beginning, twisting around like a noodle dropped on a pile of rocks. And then the trail ended again, in the middle of a vast boulder field, and Younis couldn't find it, no matter how hard he looked.

He slumped to the ground in despair, feeling exposed sitting among the rocks, open to both the sky and the valley far below. He hoped his dark clothes did not stand out against the lighter granite. The ringing in his ear was pronounced, new, and he tried to get rid of it by screwing up his eyes. When that didn't work, he opened them and searched the slope below for any signs of movement, any hint that he might have been discovered. His arm throbbed with an immobilizing pain. Distant, booming thuds echoed from the rocks and seemed to suck away the air. He longed for the cave, to simply be there, to be anywhere that would get him out from under the open sky and off the slope. His head rang as though hit with a mallet. He needed the cave, which he imagined had been custom-built for him, for his shelter, perhaps by his father or his grandfather. His imagination made it a living thing, a rescuer, an active participant in his struggle.

Perhaps he passed out. He lost track of time. Eventually, because he had no choice, he stood. His arm did not seem to be bleeding as much, but he did not dare to look underneath the cloth he kept wrapped around it. He walked around a subtle bend in the hill that did not look like anything at all when viewed from below, but which stretched farther back into a seam in the hillside, its depth becoming apparent only as he entered it. He climbed up what turned out to be a shallow gorge in the rock, mostly hidden from view when seen from below. He surveyed the landscape again. Up the hill, on the other side of this crevice, he saw a flat, shelflike protrusion balanced on the steep slope, and some outcroppings of vegetation, scrub brush and dwarf pine, and farther down the rock were tiny groves of elm and birch, tucked into a hidden part of the mountain.

The sun was descending in the western sky when he stepped around a corner, up over the shallow ledge, and onto a rocky flat, which had a clear view of a large section of the valley. A ledge, but no cave, only the mountainside covered by a heavy layer of dead coarse brush and sage. But as he looked closer, prodded around in the tangle of branches and thorns, he was unable to find the rock wall which the brush appeared to cover. Instead he found that the stone curved inward, and that the vegetation was not well attached, as he first thought, but that it came off in his hand when he grabbed it, revealing a dark recess behind.

Little by little, the branches fell away, revealing a shallow opening about the same depth as the ledge, the ledge itself serving as a kind of threshold. His imagination had turned the cave into a kind of temple, but reality was rougher. He was not disappointed, desperate as he was for any kind of shelter before the approaching night, but at the same time, the shallow depression in the rock wall did not live up to the image he had created in his mind. Judging by the dark burn marks on the ceiling and the packed earth that made up the floor, he concluded that it had been used as a shelter in the past, perhaps during an earlier war.

The sun was sinking quickly, and the temperature began to drop with it. Younis set about as best he could making the cave marginally more habitable, clearing out what brush and stone he could with his good left arm. He was no stranger to sleeping outside, although he usually had a fire during all but the warmest parts of summer. But he carried nothing with him to make a fire, no matches, no flint, and the prospect of spending the night exposed and alone without warmth terrified him.

He pushed away some stones from the cave floor, enough to create a flat area on which to lie, and dragged a fir bough to cover it as a kind of rough pallet. Then he took the dry brush he had pulled from the cave mouth and stacked it up around the rim of the ledge, to prevent the opening from being seen from below. This done, the sun dipping below the horizon, he crawled inside the cave, exhausted, and blacked out.

5

He woke shivering in the dark, the cave mouth edged by the crescent moon's silvery light. His teeth rattled together and his fingers and toes had gone numb. With tremendous effort, he stood up and walked to the entrance of the cave, moving

his limbs in an effort to regain some feeling. As he left the
cave and walked onto the rocky ledge, he was bathed by the
moon, the same wan light that anointed the great valley laid
out before him. A thousand visible stars beamed tiny versions
of the same pale cast, making everything appear to glow from
within. Gradually his limbs, though still cold, regained most of
their feeling, and his forearm throbbed. He could clearly see
his breath, which seemed to be painted with the same silver
sheen. Despite his cold and hunger, he found comfort in the
sight of it, precious as the unknowable future, as though the
concentrated energy of everything he saw were being focused
upon him, standing high up on the mountain, looking out over
all the world.

6

Jonas allows this image to linger. He has always liked this
detail, this thought: the moonlight, himself looking out on the
valley. He is not lying about it, either. At least, no more so
than anyone who tells a story. He was there. If anything, it was
more dramatic than he describes. But he can't help thinking
that maybe he is overdoing it. Perhaps he describes the moonlight once too often. As he watches Rose's face, Jonas becomes
concerned that he has gone too far.

The difficulty, he realizes, is inherent in the use of both
words and memory. Their imprecision combines to make it
nearly impossible for him to tell a true story. Even as he speaks,

he is conscious of the fact that it wasn't exactly as he describes. Had he really stopped beside the river that night, looked out into it and thought those things, or had he done that on a previous evening, and then, once again, superimposed one memory on top of another? Does he describe the river accurately, his frantic journey along it, or does he use a sort of verbal shorthand to convey to Rose the general picture, and allow her imagination to fill in the details? Is there any other way to tell her what happened?

Because what Jonas wants, after all, is not simply to describe for Rose a mountain or a cave or his desperation. What he wants is for Rose to feel something, fear or pain or anger or heartache, even if only as a semblance of the emotion he detects within himself, even as he sits in her living room and tells this version of the story. He wants her to know, needs her to know, needs to place it all into context, needs to explain himself, wants her to understand.

So he continues to talk, continues to describe for her how it was, or how he remembers it, or at least how he has convinced himself he remembers it. How scared he was, how angry, how desperate, how alone. And if it comes across as stilted or overwrought, if in his effort to commune with her, conjure for her his reality, he uses commonly held devices, if he describes once too often the strange crescent moon that lit up the world, or his shivering, or the accursed cave in which he was forced to spend the days of his youth, it is in the service of a greater purpose, and he can easily be forgiven.

7

At some point, Younis was woken by convulsions. He lay on his side at the mouth of the cave, legs drawn up and wrapped by his arms. He shivered a little more and closed his eyes, tensing his muscles in an effort to keep away the cold. He shivered again, and moved to stand up, recover some warmth through the motion of doing so. But as he put his hands to the cold earth and began to push himself up, he found that he could not do it, that he lacked the strength to lift his body. He tried again, and again, but found that he could not make himself rise. He tried to open his eyes, but found that he could not, or perhaps, he thought, with a panic suppressed by fatigue, his eyes were open but he could not see anything, or perhaps the world had simply disappeared.

The shivering stopped suddenly, replaced by a distant warmth, and Younis smiled weakly to himself. He drifted in a void, a blackness so complete that a moonless night was like broad daytime in comparison. Images confronted him and then disappeared before he could focus on them, made compelling by his inability to resolve them. He chased after them, trying desperately to focus on something, anything, and a gentle, spinning sensation took hold, rocking him back and forth, lulling him, but simultaneously making it impossible to focus on any one thing, impossible to think, impossible to move. Helpless and exposed, vague visions approaching him from all directions, he gave up trying to focus on them, let them go, and allowed himself to drift.

And then he was back in his village, where everything was as it was supposed to be, his mother walking out to the pasture at the end of the dusty road, carrying naan wrapped in cloth and hot tea, which he took, steaming, in the bright cool air. The sheep surrounded him, and he protected them with devotion, for their wool, for the warmth and the food they provided. He sipped from the earthen bowl his mother handed him, the tea sweetened and faintly spiced, and he looked up into green eyes that so readily mirrored his own. As he looked, her face changed, growing gradually lighter and lighter, as though the sun overhead were drawing itself closer to the earth. He looked around to see that everything grew brighter, less resolute: the pasture, the stone wall, the earth itself fading away, losing contrast in the light. Soon he could see only her most obvious features, her eyes and nose and mouth, her dark hair, and everything else, her skin and wrinkled brow, her arms and hands, grew brighter with each passing moment, until all he could see was light, and nothing else existed. She disappeared into it, disappeared along with everything else, everything he knew, the pasture and the sheep and the hills and the village and even the river itself, the source of all of it, everything he knew, all of it blending into a golden light that was suddenly his entire existence.

8

The light bathed him and he woke, lying on his side beside a crackling fire, covered by a thin blanket, his limbs prickling and stiff as the feeling gradually returned to them, the flame's glow wrestling with the darkness and cold. The smell of cooking food violently ignited his suppressed hunger. Squinting into the flickering light, he could make out only a shadow across the fire, a presence overwhelming the refuge in which he had been so isolated. He closed his eyes, mildly surprised to find that he was not yet dead, then opened them again, tried to focus on the figure opposite him.

"*Salaam aleikum*," said the figure.

Younis heard the words, clear and accented, oddly pronounced, but was too weak and shocked to respond, and then he lost consciousness again.

"Are you okay? Can you hear my greeting?" said the figure. "I said, 'Peace be with you.'"

Younis rubbed his head, then tried turning to get a good look at the place where the voice came from, but could not move. Gradually he brought the figure into vague focus, adjusting his vision to the harsh firelight. The man was dressed in an odd mix of local and foreign clothes, camouflage fatigues devoid of patches or insignia, a kamiz, and a pakol cap. He gazed levelly at Younis, patiently awaiting his response.

"And also with you," Younis finally replied, weakly. "And you in return? Are you well?" His voice was barely louder than a whisper.

"I am well, sir, thank you," said the man.

"You are English?" said Younis, in English.

"I speak English," said the man.

"Why are you here?"

"I guess I am lost."

9

Younis, his mind addled, tried to force his head clear and strained not just to understand the stranger's English, but to place it. He could not, as it was so dissimilar from the English he had heard his father, or anyone else, speak.

He could feel the strength flowing back into his limbs, spurred by the warmth of the fire, and abruptly he tried to stand.

"If it is not too forward, sir," began Younis, "may I ask where are you . . ." But he stumbled weakly, and fell back down to the earth.

"Have something to eat," said the man, and stepped around the fire, stopping to pick up a shallow pan that had been warming there, and offered it to Younis. "I'm afraid it's not much."

Younis shoveled the food from the pan to his mouth with

his hand. It tasted like beef and some sort of mashed vegetable, but had a plastic taste he could not place. He had to keep himself from throwing it back up out of his empty stomach. The man offered some water from an opaque bottle that faintly carried the same plastic odor.

"Are you from the village down there," asked the man, pointing his thumb over his shoulder in the direction of the valley, toward the bottom of the mountain.

Younis thought first to answer truthfully, and then thought better of it.

"No," he said. "I come from Yokshal, on the other side of the mountain," naming a village he had heard his father speak about occasionally, the home of some distant cousins, or perhaps an uncle.

"Huh," said the man, evidently either unfamiliar or unconcerned with the other village. "We must have come from opposite directions. I came up from the river."

As his eyes became more accustomed to the light, Younis could make out the man's features a little more clearly, filling in the vague outline. He was several days unshaven, with light blue eyes rarely seen in that part of the world. His left forearm was wrapped in a dirty bandage, a mirror image of the wound on Younis's right arm, and a thin cut, just beginning to heal, accented his left cheek and temple. He was well armed, a long rifle propped against a rock beside him, and the hilt of a combat knife protruded from a strap around his thigh.

"How long have you been here?" asked the man.

"I could ask you the same question," said Younis, his voice weak and rasping.

"Here?" said the man, motioning to the ground around him. "About two hours. This part of the world? Nearly a year."

"I don't know how long I have been here," said Younis, slowly gathering his strength. "I fell, injuring my arm, as you can see, and came here to this shelter because I could not walk home. But I have always lived here."

The man looked at Younis coldly, as though measuring his words, then smiled a little half smile and said, nodding at Younis's arm, "I can take a look at that, if you want. I have some supplies with me."

The wind picked up, coursing down the valley and up the steep slope, carrying with it a faint smell, gunpowder and something else, like burning hair. Twenty minutes later, Younis rode a soft cloud of morphine, the roughly stitched wound on his forearm protected from infection by an injection of antibiotics. The morphine bore him up, higher than the mountain, far away from pain or fear or sorrow or loss. How wonderful it would have been to stay on that cloud, to ride on it forever, to drift eternally, untethered. Younis was thinking these thoughts when he fell into the deepest sleep he had ever known.

10

The story, as Jonas tells it, is mostly accurate. If Rose is able to spot what he changes or leaves out, her face gives no indication. But she does not relax, does not even breathe. She waits.

"I woke in a hospital bed," he says, nodding up at the huge

portrait over the mantel, its size directly proportional to the home's grief. "I am sure that's him, but I'm sorry I can't help you any more than that."

The faint background noises—the creaking chair legs, the ticking grandfather clock—grow to fill the room's silence. Jonas sits back in his chair, but Rose remains balanced on the front of hers.

"But," she says, "there must be more."

Jonas says nothing. He bunches his shoulders in what could be a shrug, and bites his lip.

"There must be more," says Rose.

"I wish I could—"

"There must be more. You have to remember something else. I can't believe it. That's it? You just 'woke up'?"

"I know, and I'm very sorry I can't help you more."

"But maybe if you tried. Anything. What was he wearing? How badly was he hurt? Was he scared? Did he tell you anything else? I just can't believe it."

"I wish I could remember something else, something more."

"Yes, anything. Did you see him leave? Did you see where he went? Did he tell you if he had plans?"

"Look, I know how you must feel."

"You have no idea how I feel!" says Rose. "You have no idea what it's like to know that you might never see—" She wipes her cheek quickly with a tissue. "I'm sorry," she says. "Of course you do. I'm sorry. I just, well. I just miss him very much."

The sound of the clock in the corner seems to grow again to fill the room, and when Jonas speaks, he does so almost as much to drown out the sound as anything else.

"There is one thing," he says.

Rose leans even farther forward.

"I just have this image, really. This thing I remember. He had this book that he wrote in, like a diary. Quite a lot. I don't know what he put in it. But he had it. Maybe that is something."

For a long time Rose doesn't say anything. Then, almost reluctantly, she nods. "Thank you," she says. "But really, maybe you'll remember something else. Maybe you'll wake up one morning and think of something. Maybe something will just come to you. You can call me anytime, if it does. I would be grateful."

They talk awhile longer. Jonas thinks that Rose's face looks somehow older than it did when she first opened the door. She asks more questions about his time on the mountain, with her son, but he is unable or unwilling to give any further information, and she leans back, reluctantly, and allows the conversation to drift.

Which it does, meandering around Christopher's early childhood, school and friends, trailing off as its subject ages, closes in on his ultimate fate, which hovers, phantomlike, over the room. Other than seeking to discover what happened to him, Rose does not seem to have any real interest in talking about the military, or Chris's life once he entered it. It is as though the portrait on the wall was taken as his life ended, and the subsequent years turned into hazy recollections and unending sadness.

Jonas and Shakri sense that it is time to leave before anyone states the fact. The sunlight through the windows is golden, the shadows elongated, and they reach an unspoken consensus. Rose hugs them awkwardly to say good-bye as they get up, and again before they go out the door.

And then she is nearly pushing them out into the cool, late afternoon. They stand on the front step, and she holds the door open with her hand across the threshold like a gate, preventing them from reentering the house. She makes it clear they should leave, but at the same time she tells them to come back anytime they want.

COMMUNION

I

For a time, they were little more than rumors spread by children.

The imam argued that, removed as the village was from the capital and its arcane politics, the Americans could have no possible interest in it. The only contact they would ever know would come in the form of the planes seen far overhead. If Younis's father ventured to make a counterargument, that there existed a real and imminent danger, it didn't seem to make an immediate impression.

So when Azar's youngest son, who was no more than ten years old, told his father that he had watched that very afternoon as a patch of reeds along the river moved in an unnatural way, counter to the current and the prevailing mountain wind, it was written off as a figment of the youngster's imagination.

And when Jangi Shah's middle son claimed to have found a boot print in the dew-moistened earth at the base of the rise to the west of the village, he fetched his friends to go and take a look. But one of the boys stepped on it by accident, blurring the impression and making it impossible for anyone else to tell for sure what it was.

Then one evening Ahmand's nephew said that he thought he had glimpsed a parachute falling from the sky on the other side of the river. But when he was questioned further, he conceded that it could have been a kite, or maybe an old plastic bag swept along on the breeze.

In those places where the children gathered, one could perceive, if one cared to listen, in their hushed tones and joking insults, a certain skepticism about what their mothers had told them: that the Americans had come to take away naughty children who did not obey their parents, that they lurked in the dark places between the houses, waiting patiently for those who had been instructed not to go outside after sunset.

But when Ali's teenage daughter came running home at dusk one evening, closing the door quickly behind her, and explained breathlessly that she had seen a lone man stalking in the brush beside the river road, a giant of a man with brilliant blue eyes and a chest like a horse, it was finally conceded that something strange must be happening.

The most probable explanation, it was widely agreed, was that the village was suffering the hauntings of ghosts.

2

Occasionally he hears the voice of his savior.

Usually he tries to ignore it.

It comes to him when he is tired, or drunk, or asleep, or not asleep, simply lying in his bed and unable to turn his thoughts to anything else. He tries to force it to join the chorus in his head, the background noise that reminds him he is alive.

"Perhaps she is correct," says Paul. "Perhaps there is more to the story."

The voice in his head is softly accented by the Pennsylvania hills. It is gentle, and deep, and brings with it the haunted souvenirs of the past: the scent of woodsmoke and reheated rations drifting up a mountain slope, the echo of metal on whetstone as a combat knife is sharpened, the scratching sound of pencil on paper, the crackle and pop of burning cedar, the thin, high tearing noise of another blister pack being opened, another morphine-filled syringe prepared.

"Very well," says Jonas. "Perhaps there is."

With effort, he begins to talk. He tries to get it right, tries to match the words exactly, but has the familiar feeling that he is adding and subtracting, substituting what should have been said for what he fails to remember accurately. He channels the voice as best he can, feels it condense within him and propel out of him, and as he speaks, as this voice speaks through him, he feels himself take a step, as though off a cliff and into the unknown.

3

For a while we were stationed in Uganda. What we were doing there is not important. Weekends, we used to go to the wildlife pre-

serve, just to look around, see the animals. There was an agreement with the government, and we got in free.

So many animals. Animals I had never seen before in real life: giraffes, rhinos, hyenas, lions. The preserve was just a small area of land, and most of the surrounding countryside was being logged or mined. So all these animals were crowded into this little wild area, like ants on a leaf in a rainstorm.

Once, we were driving along and we came upon a woman pulled over beside the dirt trail they used for a road. She's a wildlife biologist, she says, and she's sitting there in her vehicle, staring through binoculars, off into the brush.

"Look at this," she says. I look, and for a long time I don't see anything. She hands me her binoculars. The colors there in the bush, at that time of year, well, there's really only one color, a sort of sand or tan or khaki, just lots of different shades of it, so everything blends together, the earth and the shrubs and the trees and everything, all just the color of the sand. So I'm looking at this, and I don't see anything. I'm starting to get a little frustrated, maybe, because this woman is obviously convinced that something spectacular is there.

"No," she says, "over there, a little to the left."

And then I see it.

There in the underbrush, not fifty yards away, is a lion. It's a lioness, actually, the biologist tells me. She has been watching this lioness for two days.

"A lioness," I said. "Wow, that's great."

"No," she said, "look closer."

And then I think I must have gasped, because standing there

right next to the lioness was a little baby gazelle. He was tiny, and so weak he could barely stand, his legs all skinny and sort of quivering, whether from his own weight or fear or both. Every once in a while, the lioness would reach out with one of her huge paws, wrap it around the gazelle, pull him over, and lick his face, just like a dog licking your hand. It seemed like two competing instincts were fighting it out inside of her: her urge to hunt, and her urge to mother. In response, the gazelle would nuzzle up against the lioness's side, maybe not entirely comfortable with the whole situation, but feeling, for a moment, safe.

What had happened, the biologist explained, was that two days previously, the pride's big alpha male had killed both the baby gazelle's mother and the lioness's cub.

"They're heartbroken," she said. "They've adopted each other."

"That's impossible," I said. But there I was, looking at it, unable to convince myself that it wasn't true.

We went back the next afternoon, and they were all still there: the lioness, the gazelle, and the biologist, who stayed there for days. She had never seen anything like it, she said, and she had been studying lions for years. It really affected her. She couldn't think about anything else for weeks afterward, lost her appetite, spent days alone in the bush.

The situation couldn't last. They weren't eating, and sooner or later something had to give.

It ended badly.

But I have never forgotten it. I carry it with me. Somehow, the fact that it ended is not as important to me as the fact that it happened. In a way, they're still there, now that I've seen them, *set together by chance or fate under the African sun, safe, for the moment, from the surrounding cruelty, each one's life given meaning by the other's.*

4

As soon as they are back in the car, Jonas glances through the packet Rose handed to him, and before they are even out of the neighborhood, he begins to form some initial impressions. They are copies of articles clipped from newspapers, and letters, or memos, and photographs.

The photographs hold Jonas's most immediate attention.

Some of them are black-and-white, and others have been reproduced in color, apparently printed using a newer photocopier. They present varying degrees of clarity. Some of them are more toner smudge than anything else, while others are tack-sharp. They are interspersed among printed-out e-mail and official-looking correspondence. Jonas is struck by the feeling that he has seen them before, if not these exact photographs, then images eerily similar to them. In one photo, a young Christopher stands with his arm around another soldier in front of a tank, starkly silhouetted under a blazing sky. There is a picture of him at some sort of dance or function, in a formal dress uniform, holding hands with a blond-haired girl who is nearly as tall as he is. Another shows him mud-spattered and obviously exhausted, hunched over a picnic table, but managing despite his fatigue to smile up at the camera. Still another shows him wearing a camouflage uniform, with a large duffel slung over his back, making his way up the ramp of a cargo plane.

5

Rose Henderson pushes the front door closed as Jonas and Shakri leave, then leans against the wooden frame, feeling the cool October breeze through the open living room window. Next to the front door, a tall wooden box that Christopher once dragged home from shop class holds a pair of umbrellas, angled gently away from each other. An old horseshoe, collected during one of the family's innumerable treks through the Pennsylvania countryside, hangs upturned over the doorsill. She feels suffocated as soon as the door is closed, unable to breathe deeply.

The photograph over the mantel. The folded flag on the bookshelf. She is used to them, aware she has gathered these things around her, made the decision to leave them as they were, in view, and as a result they are only occasionally difficult to look at, painful only when she thinks about them too deeply.

But there are the other objects: the boxes of toys and sports equipment hidden away in the basement, out of sight, the school papers and certificates and finger paintings in the attic. And now, to these objects, she adds a list of people. If that which is left in open sight has grown less painful over time, she cannot even think about that which is hidden away.

And then Rose is aware that she has slumped to the floor, that she sits alone in the foyer, pressing her back against the front door.

She spends a few moments trying to gather herself together, rubs her eyes with her hands, is finally able to take a breath, and stands up. She has much to do, she thinks. She grabs a short-handled spade from a bucket next to the sliding glass door that leads onto the back porch and steps into the waning rays of the thin autumn day.

The Henderson property is surrounded by a low stone wall, which Roy Henderson built before their divorce. The wall demarcates a smaller plot around the house, and a larger plot beyond, the back forty, as they always called it, although it is nowhere near so large as forty acres. The back forty is now the domain of overgrown grass, rabbits, and deer. Before he left, Christopher would occasionally mow a section of it, and, with help from the two younger boys, Matthew and Sam, pour down white lime from a large paper bag to mark out a football field or soccer pitch. Then they would stay outside, their footfalls like tiny thunderclaps, until it was so dark they could no longer see.

Rose divides her days by tasks. She writes letters in the morning, attends meetings in the afternoon, or makes phone calls, the important work of organizing the support group occupying more and more of her time. The important work. They always tell her, as if she needs to be told, how important it is. And yet she can't do it all the time, nor all by herself. She has some help, the increasingly complex work now spread among several volunteers. She hears from more and more people who want to get involved, and the group is growing, a fact she finds nearly as tragic as the fact that it exists in the first place.

It wasn't that the two other boys were unaffected, thinks Rose. Not at all. But they were young. And then time passed so quickly, as first Matthew went off to take a construction job outside the state, and then Sam started at college, the first of her boys to do so.

Someone had once told her, insensitively rather than maliciously, that at least she had her other children, implying that when you have several, the loss of one is easier to bear. But Rose knew this for the lie it was. Her other boys were doing well, and she was proud of them, loved them, but everything seemed somehow fainter after Christopher disappeared, and Rose often felt as though she had one foot in the here and now and the other foot somewhere else. Maybe another person would react better, she thinks, and then, with effort, pushes that thought, all the thoughts, away.

Between letters and phone calls and meetings, she takes out her frustration on the weeds in the backyard. She thinks about putting together something for dinner, something light, not really feeling hungry but knowing she has to keep up her strength. The sun is rapidly dropping toward the horizon, its descent chilling the air. Rose thinks about dinner, and something about the light or the crisp fall air reminds her of another dinner, at the end of another fall day not too many years ago.

They ate it around the table in the kitchen. Tacos, she thinks, piled with lettuce and tomatoes in an effort to get her family to eat at least something of the vegetable family. Roughage, she used to call it, before one night when Christopher announced he didn't like the word "roughage" because it sounded like you were going to be attacked by your salad.

After dinner there was still a little light outside, and Christopher wanted to show them something he had learned in soccer practice that afternoon. They filed out through the sliding glass door and into the backyard. It took him a few tries. He got a soccer ball and put it on the ground, placing one foot in front of it and the other behind, and with a scissor motion kicked the ball high into the air, then hit it squarely with his forehead, before kicking it again with his other foot, and they all watched it arc neatly through the autumn air, past everyone, over their heads, and smack into the graceful stone wall. He looked over at his parents and smiled. "Isn't that cool?" he said.

"Yes," said Rose, "that's fantastic."

And for just a moment, she remembers, it was.

6

When we arrived, we told them we were there to help them, but they were ambivalent. It was almost like they were bored. But then we started passing out cash, and they registered the possibilities.

One day we backed the APV up beside the central market. Skeets accidentally pressed the gas instead of the brake, and we hit a merchant's stall. It damaged the wooden booth and the awning. So Jacobs goes over and offers him something to pay for the damages. He accepts it, looks grateful. We could have just driven away. But

then the guy in the stall next to him pipes up and says that we hit
his stall, too. Sure enough, his awning is knocked over, but Gomez
swears the guy kicked it over himself. So what do you do? Jacobs
gave him some money, but less than he gave the first guy, and this
idiot gets pissed off. Starts talking about how he's going to call the
governor.

When they realized how it worked, they started applying lever-
age. We'd have locals claiming we broke their shit all the time. For
a lot of the guys, this is about when their outlook on things started
to change.

7

Jonas sits in the front seat, looking through the folder on his
lap, which entirely consumes his attention, but Shakri wants to
talk. The photocopies of news articles and pictures and letters
are spread across his lap. He glances over them, but he has the
problem with car sickness. As he tries to read, his stomach turns
and he gets nauseous. Shakri is asking him how he feels about
seeing Rose, but he doesn't want to talk about it.

He engrosses himself in the contents of the folder. Black-
and-white photographs, and letters on official stationery, army
stationery, rendered by the photocopier in shades of gray.
The late-autumn sun drops steadily, and Shakri is still asking
him questions he doesn't want to answer. He starts to sweat.
His stomach feels as though it will come up his throat any

second. Occasionally he takes a photo out of the pile to show to Shakri, who can't really see what he's trying to show her as she drives, or he tries to read aloud a section of an article for her benefit, anything to divert her attention. But he can't concentrate.

"Pull over," he says.

"What? Why?"

"Pull . . ." And then his stomach opens up and he vomits all over the inside of the car, all over the folder, the photocopies, spewing a partially digested mix of cookies and juice.

"Oh, God . . ." says Shakri, and pulls the car over fast, nearly running into the guardrail in the process. "Why didn't you tell me?"

But he is unable to answer, because he has opened the car door and is spitting the last of his stomach's contents over the buildup of cinders and ash beside the road.

"Why didn't you say something?"

"I tried," he says, breathless, "but . . . so fast."

He is wiping vomit off his chin with his hand, wiping it off however he can, trying not to get any of it on a picture of soldiers gathered in front of a row of sandbags. They pull the damp floor mat out of the passenger side of the car and dump it over the guardrail, down a small ravine beside the highway, where it lands among thousands of cigarette butts, cola bottles, and a pair of white underpants. He salvages as many pages from the packet as he can, scraping vomit off those that can be saved with the edges of those that can't.

"Do you have a paper towel or something?" he asks, and Shakri rummages around for a while in the trunk before holding up a single fast-food-restaurant napkin. He uses it as best he can to wipe down the dashboard, the seat, the armrest, but it is quickly soaked through and useless, and he tosses it over the guardrail, where it lands next to the floor mat.

They get back into the car, which smells, despite their efforts, like ammonia and grape, and pull carefully back onto the highway. Jonas says he is feeling slightly better, and Shakri alternates between asking whether he is okay and concentrating to keep herself from retching.

They drive the two hours back home, bathed in the scent of partially digested hospitality.

8

Jonas remembers the dusty road he walked back home from the schoolhouse, which was set on a hill just outside the village in a whitewashed old colonial building whose original purpose had been forgotten. He remembers being hungry, eager to get home, and the golden begonia lining the road, wild and scattered in the irrigation channels.

As he pushes open the heavy front door, he hears voices, men's voices, rare, but not unknown, a cousin, or an uncle, whose names he has long forgotten, but who were once frequent visitors. His mother is there, cleaning, putting things in order. Maybe she has been cooking, as he hopes, because his stomach has been rumbling in time to his steps. Or is this something else, another fragment recalled from another time?

Is he not combining two different memories again, conflating them into a common past?

There is no way for him to know for sure.

He is more certain about walking into the front room and seeing it transformed, the shock of finding it unfamiliar. Furnishings have been removed, the common items to which he is accustomed, the low table, and the wool rugs and thin pillows, and the ornate silver teapot that usually sits next to the door. All the banal tools of the everyday have been swept away, moved elsewhere.

In their place, groups of men, some of them familiar, some of them complete strangers, sit or kneel or squat on the balls of their feet in small circles of two and three. They huddle around little piles of dark powder heaped on the floor, or beside a stack of short lengths of pipe, or next to a large gray car battery, or over a coil of wire, wound around itself in a loose circle and resting in the corner of the room, sitting on the floor, looking for all the world like a snake.

9

They drive the rest of the way home, and Jonas disappears again into his thoughts. It's dark by the time they get back to the city and park the car. He's feeling much better, he says, but a little tired. They stop by Primanti Bros. on the way home, because Jonas insists on picking up some beer, which he says will help settle his stomach. He holds the packet Rose gave him under his arm, now damp and about three-quarters as full as it was when he received it. He buys a forty-ounce bottle and avoids Shakri's gaze as they walk out into the blue-and-yellow neon, down Forbes to her apartment.

"Is it okay if I take a shower?" he says when they get inside.

"Please," says Shakri.

He takes the oversize bottle of beer with him into the shower, the cold liquid in his throat contrasting with the hot water pouring over his head. He takes another drink. Far from settling his stomach, the beer seems to upset it more, but he manages to force it down.

10

Rose found out only later that it was all a mistake. A bureau-cratic problem. While explaining it to her, someone called it a snafu.

Years afterward, at one of the meetings, someone tells her. They are supposed to visit you first, she is told. A real person. Two people, actually, casualty officers, are supposed to come and knock on your door and explain things to you. The letter is supposed to come only later. Or maybe they are supposed to hand you the letter. But at the time, she learns, there were so many, and they couldn't keep up, and they have only so many people trained to do it, and things got done out of order.

"Even for the missing?" she says.

"Even for the missing."

"I got a letter," she says.

The day is frozen in time. She remembers that on the afternoon it arrived in her mailbox, she was baking cookies while Matthew and Sam were out in the back forty, playing football. Or perhaps baseball. Or maybe soccer. Regardless, they were outside, creating whole worlds on a sunny afternoon, while Rose baked cookies in the kitchen. Afterward, whether or not it was true, she swore that she heard the postman drive up before the cookies were finished, but that she did not want to go outside to pick up the mail just then. Not before she finished the cookies, before her sons received them, before they smiled at her with offhanded gratitude.

Later, but not just then.

Rose did not have any particular interest in the people who sent the letter, their biographies, their career paths, their motivations or ideologies. She noticed, in the same way she noticed good wallpaper, the official-looking seal on the corner of the envelope, the fine, ivory parchment. She noticed that the envelope did not have a postmark. And somehow that was when she knew.

At some point before that, she called to her two remaining sons playing in the backyard, to tell them that the cookies were almost ready, but that if they wanted any they would have to come in and wash their hands first.

They had been outside all day. They would talk about it later, with her, with each other. They would talk about how, for a brief moment, Matthew, who had just started at the high school, thought that he might be too old to be out in the backyard playing with his little brother, about how he quickly shrugged aside this thought. Sam would talk about how he knew, just knew, that this time he would be able to throw the ball clean over Matt's head, forcing him to run and get it just as he had been forced to do for about an hour.

When they heard their mother's voice, the boys were torn between eating cookies and continuing the game, but their stomachs quickly won out. They ran in through the sliding glass door that opened onto the backyard, making a show of not tracking dirt inside even as dusty bits of it fell from their shoes.

Rose had made two dozen chocolate-chip cookies. She baked them twelve at a time, on cookie sheets placed one over the other on racks in the oven. The first dozen was nearly done baking when she called to the boys in the backyard, and she deftly formed the second dozen from clumpy balls of dough using two floral-handled tablespoons. As the boys came inside, she pulled the first batch out of the oven with mitted hands, and she reminded them not to get dirt all over the floor.

The two children sat at the kitchen table, each with a glass of milk that she poured from the carton in the refrigerator, and they waited expectantly for her to bring them a large, ivory plate of chocolate-chip cookies. She baked them once every couple of weeks, and when she did there was a minor celebration in the house. Even Roy got excited, and was known to come home from work early, if he could, just to rescue a cookie or two from his voracious sons.

Several years after receiving the letter, Rose will remove one of the five chairs from around the kitchen table. She will not give any explanation, and the missing chair will never be mentioned again.

But for now the bright sun streamed in through the window, and the steam from fresh-baked cookies rose through it. The two boys sat around the kitchen table and bantered, while Rose carried the plate over to them. As she set it down, she heard the mail truck rattle to a stop outside, noticed the silence of its stopping, but she did not go outside to get the mail immediately, did not yet step out into the October sun, did not yet feel its warmth on her arms.

Under the table, one of the boys kicked the other. The other yelled out, and Rose just smiled as she pretended to take back the plate of cookies. Outside, the mail truck abruptly started its engine, drove away down the street, its fading rattle filling the neighborhood with the sound of its mandate. There was a brief moment of silence, until both boys realized that there was no way she would really take back this gift, this memory they would have for the rest of their lives.

11

Jonas hears a knock at the door.

He has lost track of how long he has been in the shower, and Shakri knocks again and asks if he is all right.

"Fine," he says, and fills the empty beer bottle absentmindedly with water from the showerhead. He hears the phone ring, and knows from the tone of Shakri's voice that it is her mother.

Shakri talks to her mother frequently. Her mother, father, and brother are all doctors, as Shakri will be one day. She will be just like her parents, who still live in India, and her brother, in New York.

Photographs of the family—on vacation somewhere exotic and palm-lined, or visiting her once during the winter, gathered around a snowman on a white Pennsylvania day, looking like bundled-up raisins on a sugar-frosted cake, or standing in front of the Taj Mahal, tourists in their native land, or hunched with aunts and uncles and cousins over a board game in a comfortable family room—clutter Shakri's bookshelves and tabletops. When he first visited her apartment, Jonas stood transfixed by the images of Shakri's abundant family. But now he does not really look at them. He finds it too much like staring into a floodlight, the portraits and casual snapshots painting in stark relief his own want.

He keeps a portion of his heart to himself. Although he wants to do more, he finds himself loving her only halfway. He tells himself it is because he is young, too young to freely give away his heart. He tells himself it is because he needs to focus on his studies, or because of his friends, who do not always meet with her approval.

But he suspects there are larger reasons for holding back, reasons related to loss, related to the dangers inherent in loving anything fully, related to the speed with which it might be taken away.

He drinks unthinkingly from the beer bottle, and spits out what he suddenly realizes is warm shower water.

He suspects there are still bigger reasons.

He loves her only halfway. The half he gives basks in it, soaks it up. The half he gives is covered in light. But he knows that there is a part of himself that must never be shown, that could never be loved, an animal part consumed by violence and rage and survival, a part he keeps locked away behind a heavy door.

In part, he loves her only halfway for his own protection, his wounded past, his fragile heart. But mostly he holds back because, deep down, underneath everything, below his thoughts and his movements and even his breath, he hears a knock at that door, low and incessant, and he knows that were it ever opened, were it ever to escape, she would be the first to get hurt.

12

What if you become convinced that, even though you are there to help them, the locals are not only unappreciative, but might actively hate you? What if you start calling all the locals hajjis? What if you start to see them less and less as human beings and more and more as things to be categorized as either very threatening or less threatening? What if your SAW gunner accidentally pops off a round or two in the general direction of a crowd of hajjis who have gathered for some purpose you don't fully understand, but don't like the look of? What if you all start popping off at the slightest provocation? What if you start looking for provocations? What if you start to feel bored when your weapon is silent?

13

For a long time after she received the letter, Rose carried on as though it had never arrived. Her two boys still lived at home, and she was still married. She had activities to keep her busy. She attended PTA meetings. She bought groceries. With perhaps the mildest hint of desperation, she hacked at the weeds that seemed always on the verge of overgrowing the wall in the backyard. She drank coffee with friends.

And when anyone would ask, as they regularly did, whether she had received any news of Christopher, she would smile and say, "Not yet," as though she had just been asked about her tax refund, or a new pair of jeans she had ordered by mail.

And then, at some point, she realized that he was not coming back. Perhaps it was when she went into his room and noticed, as if for the first time, the accumulation of dust on the dresser and shelves. Maybe it was when she looked up from the casserole she had just removed from the oven and realized that his chair at the kitchen table had not been used in years. Perhaps it was the day she saw that the stacks of unopened mail she had been saving for him filled three large boxes.

Not that she accepted his death, per se, merely that she accepted that she would most probably never see him again.

She had been told that once she arrived at the point of acceptance, she would be able to move forward. It would mark a turning point. And they were correct, whoever it was who told her this. It did mark a turning point. But it was not the kind of turning point she had expected. She had come to think of her life as being on hold. She had an inkling that once she reached the point of acceptance, everything could finally begin again. But looking back on it, she realizes that rather than marking the point her life restarted, the day she finally accepted loss marked the point when it all fell apart.

14

You probably know a little bit what it's like. If you've ever shot a gun, even if you've ever used a slingshot, or a bow and arrow, anything like that. You see something out there, a bottle, or a tin can, something far away from you, something that looks to be totally unconnected to you, and you aim at it, pull the trigger, let go of the stone, and the thing you aimed at explodes, disappears.

Now, imagine that times a hundred, times a thousand. We use really big guns. Bombs. Mortars. It's alluring. That's power. Real power. You see a car out there, you see a truck, you see a building, you see a whole fucking village.

Gone.

15

Out of the shower at last, he finds a clean pair of his own jeans and a shirt, left on a previous visit, which Shakri has folded and placed on a stand outside the bathroom. He puts them on, then tells Shakri he's going for a walk.

"Why don't you stay here?" she says.

"I need to think," he says.

And then he's out the door and alone with his thoughts and his footfalls on the rough concrete of the sidewalk.

He feels a pleasant numb sensation in his arms, and out of habit he plays a game with himself in which he tries not to step on the cracks in the battered pavement. Whether from playing this game or not, he has developed a half fear of the cracks, a sort of ridiculous phobia, as though stepping on a crack will open a chasm in the sidewalk through which he will fall. In his mind, the game assumes larger significance.

Stupid, he thinks. Silly thoughts.

And yet he can't help but notice that he is good at it, that he has always been good at it. Good at avoiding pitfalls, avoiding problems, even imaginary problems, like cracks in the cement.

The cracked sidewalk leads Jonas to the house on Adams Street in which Hakma rents a tiny bedroom.

"You look awful," says Hakma.

"Thanks," says Jonas, as he steps into the sparse room that Hakma uses as a bedroom, study, kitchen, and dining room. Over the single bed, Hakma has tacked up a map of the world large enough to take up most of the wall. Large-headed pins protrude from various points on the map's surface, like tiny mushroom clouds. Jonas had once asked whether they marked places Hakma had visited.

"No," Hakma had said. "Each pin is a place where I have a relative."

Close to the geographical center of the map is an oblong circle drawn in thick black marker. The circle takes up portions of Turkey, Syria, Iran, and Iraq, and is labeled "Kurdistan." Hanging on the wall opposite the map is the Kurdish flag, green-and-white-and-red-striped, a bright yellow sun taking up most of the field.

"I called you earlier," says Hakma. "You were out?"

"Yes," says Jonas.

"Where'd you go?"

"Hey, tell me again about your flag."

"Really?"

"Sure."

"Well, as I may have mentioned to you previously, it is made up of three stripes, which, from bottom to top, are green, white, and red, with a large golden sunburst in the middle."

"And tell me again, what do those colors represent?"

"I'm glad you asked. The green stripe represents the land itself, verdant, fertile, the cradle of . . ."

"Is it not mostly desert?"

"It is not. It is verdant and fertile. The white band represents peace, which is what every Kurd wants, the right to live peacefully within the borders of our ancestral homeland."

"Uh-huh."

"And the red band, at the top, represents . . ."

"The blood of the people?"

"The red band represents the blood of the people, their struggle for a homeland free of foreign domination. And the sunburst in the middle is yellow, representing light and power, and it has twenty-one rays, which is important for specific religious reasons."

"What sort of religious reasons?"

"It's, um, the number, twenty-one, is the number of, um, true purity. I think."

"Well, it's a beautiful flag," says Jonas.

"It is beautiful, isn't it?"

"It is."

They stand and look at the flag for what seems to Jonas to be a long time.

"Listen," says Jonas at last, "do you fancy getting a drink?"

"I thought you'd never ask," says Hakma.

They grab their jackets and go out the front door, and the cracked cement sidewalk leads them several blocks farther downtown, to Wilson's, where they find a few more acquaintances already gathered together in a large corner booth.

Trevor carries a pyramid of pint glasses to the faux-wood table, the top of which is already covered with wet rings.

"Here's to Kurdistan," says Hakma, and out of habit, they all raise their glasses and drink.

16

In the photograph's background is a large, square limestone building with ornately carved columns and a frieze over the entrance. It looks almost classically Greek. It is pockmarked with bullet holes, and parts of it, the sharp corners, the most delicately carved figures, lie crumbled around its base. The building is the least noticeable thing in the image, the foreground of which is dominated by a soldier who may be Christopher. He wears dark sunglasses and a uniform of sand-colored camouflage the exact same hue as the shot-up building behind him. His helmet, same color, is emblazoned with sergeant's stripes, and he carries a long gun, pointed down, his finger carefully laid along its side, away from the trigger.

The soldier who may be Christopher looks down at a dark-haired boy who appears to be in his early teens, a tightly wound *lugee* wrapped around his head, and a billowing white cloth around his shoulders, tied on top of a blue-and-white-striped T-shirt. They are obviously talking, the boy looking off into the middle distance, and his hands seem to be absently twirling the fringe of the cloth. The soldier, who stands well over a head taller than the boy, is looking down at him with an earnest expression barely discernible behind his large, nearly black sunglasses. It is as though he is trying to convince the boy of something.

"Do not be afraid," he seems to be saying. "We are here to help."

17

For a time, Rose cursed the sun.

She stayed awake all night. She went to sleep at sunrise and tried to remain unconscious as long as she could. She stopped showering. She stopped taking care of Roy and the two remaining boys. They were also suffering. She knew it. But they could rot for all she cared. No, she thought, that was far too harsh. She didn't mean it. She didn't want to lose them, too. But they required so much, and she simply didn't have the energy to devote to keeping them. It was, she found, no easier to lose one just because you had others.

She made occasional, heartfelt efforts to move on. She joined a bowling league. She didn't know why. A friend had joined, and in a fit of optimism, Rose signed up, too. It was a silly idea. She hadn't been bowling since she was a girl, when the owner of the local bowling lane hosted all-night bowling parties on the weekend, locking the doors so that parents knew where their children would be. She would stay up all night long with her friends. But she remembered that it wasn't about the bowling; it was about just being there, surrounded by everyone. She remembered that it was happy.

She went bowling with the league twice, but couldn't muster the energy for a third outing. It required, she felt, too much.

So she stayed in bed for days. She lay in her room with the curtains drawn. And when the sun dared to filter through them, to brighten the room, she pulled the covers over her head, cursing its audacity for shining on a world in which Christopher wasn't even there to see it.

18

At some point, Jonas passes out. The next morning he wakes up and has no idea where he is. He does not remember the previous night, cannot recall leaving Wilson's, nor what he did afterward.

He sits up with a start, and finds that he is in his own bed, his own room. Rain rattles against the windowpanes. He does not remember finding his way back to his apartment, does not know how he even managed to dig out his house keys and get in the door. His head roars.

Through the fog in his head, he realizes that the phone has been ringing.

He decides he will try something, something he has not tried since he was very young, since he used to go to the mosque, since he happened one day as a child to meet a strange monk in red robes, who taught him how.

He takes the blanket off the bed, folds it into quarters, and places it on the floor. He remembers that he used to stay in the mosque after prayers, sitting on the prayer rugs. He kneels down on the folded blanket, sits back on his calves, closes his eyes. Everyone else was so eager to leave after prayers that they practically ran to put on their shoes, find a football, or run down the narrow streets. But he sat, waiting.

He straightens his back, breathes in, breathes out. He concentrates on his breath. But his head throbs with each heartbeat, and before long his legs have fallen asleep and gone numb, and his stomach rumbles.

Frustrated, he stands up, goes into the bathroom, and takes a shower. He is filled with good intentions. Today will be the day, he thinks. It will be different. He will get some breakfast, and then he will go to the library. There are midterm exams coming up. He will call Shakri, tell her he is all right, tell her where he has been, explain his newfound focus, share with her his determination.

Out of the shower, he sits down on the edge of the bed. His initial burst of energy has worn off. He is tired. His headache has transformed into a dull weakness in his neck and shoulders. The rain beats against the windows, and he is disheartened at the thought of going out into it. He yawns. Perhaps he will rest his eyes, just for a moment. A short nap, and then he will be able to think clearly.

He lies down on the bed, and within minutes, he is fast asleep.

19

Friday, October 7 (AP)—U.S. officials announced today what they called a "highly successful" raid against insurgent targets. The action, which officials say occurred last night, resulted in the deaths of at least fourteen enemy fighters and the capture of ten others, as well as the acquisition of "valuable intelligence information." News on American casualties was not immediately available, although at least two American soldiers are thought to be among those injured. A military spokesman promised that further information would be released in the coming days.

20

And then Rose was angry. The support group was begun out of anger as much as anything. It felt unjust. Something had been taken from her, and she had not been compensated. She felt as though she had been robbed. She wondered almost seriously whether she could sue.

It started by accident, when she saw an interview on a local public-access television show with the father of a boy who had gone off to war and been killed. Friendly fire, it had been called. He said he was unable to get the whole story, and was frustrated. He seemed angry, but calm, focused, pointed. When a caller to the program questioned his patriotism, told him that he was denigrating the memory of his son by questioning his mission, he carefully, calmly pointed out that when the caller had sacrificed one of her own loved ones, she would perhaps be entitled to that opinion, although he doubted very much that she would still feel that way, and that, in the meantime, she could go to hell.

Rose got in touch with him, contacting him through the TV station. They had coffee. He had been trying to organize other families, apply some pressure and learn the truth, and Rose admired that he had given his pain a focus. Roy seemed to want to pretend that it had never happened, that the hole in their lives could be papered over with work and silence. Here was someone who not only faced tragedy, but used it to reach out to others.

Over dinner, the man explained that he was trying to build a critical mass. "They only respond to pressure," he said. "If they think there is going to be a big stink about it, if they fear for their careers, they will talk. But if they think you are on your own, they try to dismiss you as unstable, or damaged."

Rose made the decision almost without realizing it. It started with a visit to a neighbor, a few blocks over, who had lost a son. The next day she described the visit to the man she had met through the TV show. She described the grief that had filled the room, the overwhelming pain, but also her own sense of pride, of exhilaration at finally doing something.

Before she knew it, she was writing letters to families in other parts of the state, then to her congressman, her senator, the Defense Department, the White House. Soon she was hosting groups in her home. Soon she had a purpose.

21

A few nights later Jonas blacks out again, and when he wakes up he is kneeling on the floor in the hallway outside his apartment, unable to find his keys.

Another time, he blacks out and wakes up in the park by the river, next to the Fourteenth Street bridge, waves gently lapping the shore under a pink dawn. He wakes up in the back of a strange car, parked outside a blue clapboard house, and he gets out of the car and starts walking. He wakes up in the end zone of a football field. Often, relieved, he wakes up in his own bed. To his mild amazement, he never wakes up in a gutter. Once, he wakes up in the crook of a thick tree, his legs straddling the branches, the pattern of the bark imprinted on his cheek. He wakes up in the firm grasp of a large bouncer, moments before being hurtled out through the back door.

These awakenings are enumerated, transformed into stories, to be told and retold, as they all sit around a table somewhere, and raise their glasses, and laugh.

22

And then maybe they plop you down somewhere, give you a mission, like a bite-size chunk, something you can digest. Patrol this area. Or take over that house. Search this ravine. Something you can get your head around, something that sounds simple. Protect this convoy. For that period of time, all of reality is supposed to fit into that mission; those three or five or ten words sum up the entirety of your existence. Recon that village. And it almost always goes pretty well. Not perfect. Never perfect. But usually, you go out and you do your mission and everyone comes home and then you're eating a burger in the food hall.

But let's say one time it doesn't go well. Not well at all. Let's say one time you let your guard down, or your CO gets distracted.

Or maybe nobody screws up. Maybe everyone does exactly what they're supposed to do, exactly the way they're supposed to do it, but you just get outsmarted this time. They lay a perfect trap. Maybe you're in a village and everyone's doing their job the way they're supposed to, and there are women and children around. (Which is supposed to be a good sign, by the way. They tell you to always look to see what the women and children are doing. They're smarter than you, and if they suddenly disappear, you know something's up.)

But maybe they just get the better of you that day. Maybe there are women and children all over the place and despite that, all of a sudden maybe your point man is lying on the ground bleeding from the neck. And maybe you hear those little snaps, like a million tiny flags cracking in the wind, only you know they're not flags. They're bullets breaking the sound barrier as they pass by your head. And then maybe Jacobs goes down, like he's decided to take a nap. And then all of a sudden you are certain of only two things: that you are not invincible, and that you would rather be anywhere in the world except here.

23

The phone rings, and reluctantly Jonas picks it up.

"Hello?" he says.

"Hello, Jonas?" Her voice is eager, nervous, but tries to cover itself with a tranquil veneer.

"Yes," says Jonas.

"It's Rose. Rose Henderson. I just wanted to call and say hi, you know, and to, you know, find out if you might have had a chance to think a little bit more. If you can remember."

"Hi, Mrs. Henderson, hello. Well, I am not really sure what to tell you, ma'am, that I have not already said."

"Oh, well, anything really. Anything. I would be interested in hearing anything."

"Yes, ma'am, I know. You have said that before. And I absolutely promise you, again, that I would call you. If there's anything, I mean."

"I know you will. And I'm really sorry to keep, you know. I don't mean to pester you. It's just, if there's anything."

"I know, ma'am. And believe me, I will. I absolutely will. I promise."

"I know, I know. And really, I want you to know that it could be just anything, you see. It might be something that you don't think means a thing, that maybe doesn't seem very important. And to you maybe it isn't; maybe to you it's just some silly little detail that you wouldn't normally even acknowledge. But to me. Well, it would just mean the whole world to me."

24

He remembers the ruins of a stone fortress on the road outside the village, a caravanserai. They play there, he and his younger sister, Miriam. Miriam the delicate, he remembers, the grace-ful, transformed in his memories into a glowing presence that trailed him around through childhood. Sometimes, he remembers, his elder brother, Sirhan, came along as well, but not very often.

Later, he will read about them in *The New Book of Knowledge* encyclopedia, the string of inns or rest stations that were built beside roads branching out along the vast network of the Silk Road, stretching from Shanghai to Colombo to Cairo to Vienna.

But as yet he is ignorant of the stone fort's original purpose, and so they are free to turn it into whatever they want it to be: a manor house on a plantation or the royal court in Xianyang, or the Palace of Versailles, or an Aztec pyramid. The pile of rocks is anything they want it to be.

And so it is that one day they find themselves touring the Taj Mahal, or scaling Mount Everest, or climbing the turrets of King Arthur's castle, and they round a corner and there they are, crouched against a low wall, a group of young men, bearded, with long guns slung casually over their shoulders. Sirhan is among them. They smoke something from scraps of rolled-up newsprint, and they stand suddenly when they notice that they have been seen.

Sirhan strides over to them. He stands nearly two heads taller than Younis, and his eyes are deeply bloodshot, the pupils contracted to pinpoints.

"You should not be here," he says, his voice gravelly and low.

Younis is about to say something in response, tease him, or challenge his right to tell them what to do. But then he sees that this person before him, looking like his brother and sounding like his brother, has been replaced by someone else, someone with eager eyes and a hard voice.

Younis reaches down and grabs Miriam's wrist. "Let's go," he says, backing away, unwilling to turn his face from the group of men, unwilling to allow them out of his sight. But Miriam pays no attention, and crouches down to pick up another colored stone she has spotted in the dust.

"I said let's go," says Younis, and yanks her arm, pulling her up to her feet. She cries out, but Younis refuses to let go, moves her so that she stands behind him, and backs them both away from the group of men, some of whom now smile in a way that makes him wish he could move much more quickly.

25

And then it's early November, the first truly cold night of the season, the smell of snow on the air, their breath turning to pale smoke under the street lamps, the welcome warmth of Shakri's apartment, and Jonas punches the wall in her living room.

Her first reaction is to laugh.

He had been out drinking with Hakma at Wilson's; and Shakri met him there and walked with him to her apartment. He had been eager to see her.

During the walk, under bare, shadowed trees half-lit by street lamps, maples and oaks stripped of all but their most tenacious leaves, both of them cold despite walking briskly, because until then the day had been warm and they wore only light jackets, she starts in on him again.

"How much time do you think you spend drinking with

Hakma?" she says. Her face wears the blank and open expression she uses when she is trying to make a point. It is an expression with which he has become familiar.

"Oh, please, just do not start."

"No, really, I want to know."

"Not so much."

"Really? Because I make it to be every night this week."

"I had literature class on Monday night."

"So what are we, Thursday? That's four out of five nights, Jonas. How much money do you think you spend?"

"But Wilson's is cheap."

"You have this tremendous opportunity. Look at what you have been given. You've got—"

"What I've been *given?*"

"You've got the chance to do something amazing, to be an amazing person, and you piss it away in a bar with that angry Kurd."

By this time they have arrived at her apartment. Shakri fumbles through her purse for her keys and finally gets the door open. But the whole time she keeps at him, reminding him of all he is throwing away.

"Look," she says as they walk into her living room. "I know you've had a rough time."

"A rough time?"

She starts to say something else, but Jonas cuts her off.

"What would you know of a rough time? You've had everything handed to you."

"That's not true and you know it! And you also know you can't wallow like this."

He doesn't really know how it happens. He feels the anger creep up his back, rising in him, an almost physical force, or something tangible he can touch. He feels it consume him, blocking out everything else. He feels it. He is momentarily convinced that Shakri is deliberately bringing it out, seeking it, wanting it. He convinces himself that it fulfills some need in her.

The act itself doesn't exist, only its aftermath. Jonas doesn't even realize what he is doing until he draws back his fist and punches the wall next to the front door.

To his astonishment, Shakri laughs, albeit a little nervously.

"Oh, no," she says, her accent fluttering. "No, you don't, you melodramatic git. There is no way I'm going to start living in a country-and-western song."

He regrets it almost instantly. He has punched a spot on the wall next to the front door, and realizes only afterward that he has hit not the dramatically breakable drywall, but the solid wood of the doorframe. His hand throbs, and he thinks he may have felt something snap in his wrist. The spot on the wall shows no sign of having been touched. His anger dissipated, his hand rapidly beginning to swell, he sits down on the couch.

"I, um . . ." he says, holding his wrist, "I think I really may have hurt myself."

"You idiot," says Shakri gently. "Let me see."

She sits next to him on the couch and runs her hand down his arm and over the long, pale scar on his forearm.

"So now I finally know," she says. "I finally know how you got that."

"You finally know," he says.

"I mean the truth," she says, meeting his eyes. "Right? And not that rubbish about being swept over a waterfall, or falling out of an apple tree, or fighting a lion, or defusing a bomb, or . . . what was that other one, the one you told Trevor?"

"Training accident with a peregrine falcon."

"Yeah, that. How did you ever come up with that?"

She touches his swollen wrist, and he winces at the contact.

"That's really swollen," she says.

"I think I might have broken something," he says.

Shakri stands, goes to the closet, and puts on a heavy coat, then hands Jonas his jacket. "Come on," she says. "My friend Mira is on call in the medical center."

"Mira?" says Jonas. "She hates me."

"Yeah," says Shakri. "If it is broken, she will be happy to set it."

Reluctantly, Jonas pulls on his jacket, easing it over his throbbing hand, and in a gust of chill air they are out the door and back into the cold night.

26

Things went downhill fast. After the ambush we didn't care. We got sloppy. We lost something. Inhibitions, I guess. It gets easier; that's for sure. Maybe we lost a little discipline. And then we started losing more guys.

First it was Marin, on point in some village, and he just lay down like he'd decided to take a nap. Then, right after that, Landon tripped an IED and literally disintegrated.

Then a truck ran over Margold. No joke. It's almost funny to think about it, if it weren't so awful. He was on his back underneath the APC, because we thought a tie-rod was broken, and he was checking it, and damn if that rig didn't just roll backward, right overtop of him. Squashed his chest flat, broke his back. We scrambled to lift it off, but there was no way.

Then, back in the zone, we had this big discussion about it. I mean, come on. You go off to war and get killed because a truck you're fixing rolls over you? You could do that in your own backyard. I had already started thinking it was fate. You showed up and you lived or you died and there was just nothing you could do to alter it. But some of the guys said that they thought it was just chance, all totally random. And we got into it a little. We were pretty upset, which, let's face it, is weird for such a high-brained discussion, fate versus chance, but somebody shoved somebody against a wall, I remember that, and there we were arguing and jabbering about our stretch of bad luck. And someone said it, said, "Well, you know, fuck it. We're cursed."

And everyone went quiet, like a secret that everybody knew but didn't dare say had been spoken out loud. And a couple of guys laughed, but someone else got really angry, said, "Shut up; don't ever say that again."

And it's true. You've got to nip that kind of thing in the bud. But it was too late. It was already out there. A unit gets that kind of thing into its head, that it's cursed, and it's useless. One of two things happens. Either they get mutinous, refuse to go out, or maybe go out and dig in somewhere, refuse to do anything, or else they snap.

We snapped.

27

In the morning, Rose writes letters, often waking before dawn in the cold house and putting a kettle on to boil water for tea before settling into the rocking chair in the large-windowed addition Roy built before the divorce. *Dear Timothy,* she writes, in a graceful, flowing script on a sheet of cream stationery, writing by hand because she is still not entirely comfortable writing on the laptop that sits next to the printer upstairs. *You don't know me, but you served with my son.*

Roy bought her both the laptop and the printer, and checks in on her occasionally, as she does on him. Separated after Christopher disappeared, now divorced, they are friends, of a sort. While Rose had founded the support group, Roy had seemed capable of carrying on as though nothing had happened, and Rose resented him. So she funneled into her work with the group all of the energy and attention that had been squeezed out of the marriage.

Even now, though friendly, they are vaguely wary of each other, each blaming the other in part for the loss of their son, even as they each know how irrational it is to do so.

I am writing because I have organized a group of veterans and

*their families, anyone who has lost friends or loved ones in the line
of duty.*

Many of the soldiers and family members she contacts
never get back to her, and she is not offended or put off by this.
Quite the opposite: She finds it completely understandable,
assuming that they want as much distance as possible from the
past. But this is the opposite of her own reaction, and that of
those who do get in touch with her, those who share a need to
be close to others who have had similar experiences.

*We are a group of over one hundred family members, friends,
and comrades who have lost loved ones.*

She never pesters or cajoles, and she is careful not to go on
too much about her own loss. Her mission, she feels, is simply to be there, to be in touch, offering to those affected the
opportunity for fellowship.

28

Jonas wakes up in pitch darkness to the sound of Shakri's
screams.

They are being hunted. He lies on his back, hiding with
Shakri next to him. She screams into his ear, his good left
ear, so that he can hear nothing aside from her screams. He
can't move, can't sit up. They are surrounded. He tries to sit up
again and smacks his head against something hard. He tries to
keep them alive.

"I don't understand you, Jonas!" Shakri sounds frantic, desperate. "What are you saying?"

It is her voice, but it feels unfamiliar. It is as though she is speaking to someone else, calling him a different name, in a different language, and he registers it merely as a kind of nuisance that threatens to prevent him from doing what needs to be done, and which, more important, threatens to give them away. He is trying to save her, and he needs her to shut up and let him do it.

"Wake up, Jonas, oh, please wake up!"

She is crying now, trying to keep her voice calm, sounding as though she is reasoning with a mugger or a rapist. He wraps his arm around her neck and clasps his hand tightly over her mouth.

He finds that he cannot move his legs, that they feel bound, and he reaches down the length of his thigh with the hand that is not holding shut Shakri's mouth and gropes around to try to figure out what is restraining him.

It feels like bedsheets.

Then he takes a breath. Slowly, he releases his grip on her mouth.

In the darkness, he reaches up, grabs hold of the wooden slats, and pulls himself out from under the bed. He slides out of the sheet and blanket, which have wrapped themselves around his legs. Then he reaches down and tries to help Shakri crawl shakily out, as well, but she pushes away his hands.

He stands beside the bed, his bare chest bathed dimly by the light from the street lamp outside the window, which barely

penetrates the darkness of Shakri's bedroom. He is soaked with
sweat, and the cool air brings out goose bumps on his arms
and legs. He hears nothing but a ringing sound in his good ear.
He opens his mouth to say something, then closes it again.
When sounds finally emerge from his mouth, they are raspy
and forced, his voice catching in his throat.

"I don't . . ." he says. "What happened?" he says. He says, "I
didn't mean . . ." and, "Are you okay?"

Shakri is curled fetally on the other side of the bed, practically as far away from Jonas as she can get while remaining
in the same room. She holds the side of her head as though
in pain, and Jonas suddenly realizes that he injured her as he
dragged her underneath the bed. Her body shakes, but she is
quiet except for an occasional sob or rapid intake of breath. He
crosses the room and sits next to her.

"I thought we were going to be killed," he whispers, and
reaches out gently to put his hand on her leg.

"Don't," she says. "Just don't," she says. "Just please don't
touch me."

29

*What if, a few days later, you find them? What if you find them
a week after they kill your point man while you're patrolling some
stretch of highway outside some godforsaken village? What if you
find them a few days after you lose someone else, vaporized by*

*an IED right outside that same godforsaken village? What if you
are absolutely certain that some of the locals know them, know who
did it, who it was that killed your friends? What if you then get some
intel? What if you get confirmation? What if you suddenly know
where they are?*

30

The next day it rains, and Rose can do no work in the backyard,
so she reads some e-mail she has managed to print out from the
computer, or she makes some phone calls, or she stares through
the window at the giant drops flooding the small porch outside
the front door.

She can still picture them standing there, framed by the
doorway, soaking wet, the three of them, clustered around a
red wooden wagon, and the thought makes her smile. They
wear their dripping, oversize ponchos, their rubber boots as,
behind them, the rain turns the front yard to mud.

Christopher had organized them into a team. He and Matthew were supposed to push the wagon and tuck the newspapers behind the subscribers' screen doors, while the baby,
Sam, sat in the wagon, pulling papers out from under a folded
tarp and stuffing them into plastic bags. But Sam couldn't keep
up as the houses rolled by, and then it really started to rain.
Though he is still years away from being old enough to drive,
Christopher wants to borrow the car. "Just in the neighborhood," he says.

"Come on," says Rose. "I'll drive you."

They make nearly a hundred dollars a week from the paper route, which they split among themselves and spend on toy action figures and slushies and model rockets.

"They should save some of it," says Roy.

"They'll have time to save plenty of money later," says Rose.

They roll the dripping wagon into the garage, load the damp newspapers into the trunk of the car. Matthew and Sam climb into the backseat, and Rose closes the door before whispering something to Christopher, who stands quietly next to the car.

"What were you thinking?" she asks, annoyed despite herself at having to drive them around. She speaks to him as though gently rebuking a confidant. "You know Sam isn't big enough to keep up with you two."

Christopher fixes her with his striking blue eyes. "It was just an idea," he whispers back, before he gets into the car. "I thought it would work, but I was wrong. I'm ready to move past it if you are."

31

Jonas leaves Shakri in thought before he does so in action. He has suspected he would have to. Maybe from the beginning. He has known he must. It is for her own good.

He stops calling. He avoids places he knows she may be. At first he tells himself that it is only temporary, only until he can get himself sorted out.

He knows he owes her an explanation. He considers calling her, talking to her, giving her the chance to convince him otherwise. Partly he wants to tell her why; partly he also wants to be proved wrong. Partly he is afraid of being proved wrong.

He tells himself it's only temporary. He has to work through some things. He tells himself they will get back together after he has had some time, after he gets rid of this thing inside that consumes him. He tells himself that it will be safe for her then, that they will be better than ever. But he fears that none of this is true.

In the end, he picks a time he knows she will not be at home, and he calls and leaves her a message. In the message, he explains to her the reasons he does not contact her: that he is protecting her, that it would not do for her to be with someone like him, that it is not safe, that she does not really know him, that she deserves much better, that he is capable of horrendous things.

32

"What happened to the gazelle?" asks Younis, the wind blowing more gently now, up the mountain behind him. "You know, with the lion, what happened?"

The silence of the night is broken only by the crackling of the fire, the scrape of steel on whetstone, the wind bearing up the slope, and, eventually, by a softly accented voice, almost reluctant to speak.

"Life's cruel sometimes," Christopher says. "It was fast, at least. That was the only good in it."

33

"Here's to Kurdistan," says Hakma, lifting his glass.

"You need a new toast," says Jonas.

It's a Wednesday night, and he is back at Wilson's.

"Never," says Hakma. "I will toast the motherland until the day I die."

Wilson's is empty except for one old guy at the bar, and they sit alone in a booth near the front. The beer looks clear and full, the cold glass in his hand, and he can't wait to taste it.

"Well, then, you need a follow-up."

"Aha," says Hakma. "Nothing wrong with toasting other things after the motherland." He thinks for a moment, and then lifts his glass again. "Here's to my enemies' enemies, who are my friends."

"Very original."

"Got something better?"

Jonas thinks for a moment, raises up his glass, pauses as if in sudden meditation, opens his mouth as if to speak, and then drinks down the entire glass, lifting his hand to order another before it is even completely empty.

The evening settles into a familiar pattern. Condensation from the pint glasses wets rings on the tabletop, and Hakma periodically wipes at them with a soggy napkin. The old man who has been at the bar since before they came in yells something at the bartender, who tells him, in tones gentler than the words, to pipe down or go home. Wilson's is known for nothing if not cheap beer, but when the bartender finally brings their bill, they are stunned by the tab.

"I don't have it," says Hakma.

"Don't look at me," says Jonas.

The room sways gently now that they have stopped talking. Jonas is content to sit there, comfortable in the booth, for the foreseeable future. Then he looks up to see that the bartender has disappeared into the back room, and he is suddenly all action.

"Let's bolt," he says.

Hakma looks at him for a moment, processing the options. "Yeah, okay."

Without even being aware of having made the decision to do so, they're up and out the door like they own it, like it's obvious, and before they really know it they are out into the neon night, rushing down the street through the chill air. Jonas expects shouts or sirens to hit him in the back, but there's nothing, just footfalls and traffic. He feels invincible.

They walk quickly down a side street and head up the hill toward the stadium. Close to the top they pass an apartment building, and Hakma says, "Hey, check this out."

He walks over to the building's side entrance, a glass door with a thin metal bar across the front serving as a handle.

"This is pretty cool. I discovered it a few weeks ago."

The door swings open easily at his push, and they slip into a dim hallway and through a large metal security door, which is also unlocked. Their footsteps echo from the concrete and steel in the stairwell as they climb six floors to the top, where another steel security door opens to put them on the roof.

"I have no idea why they don't lock it," says Hakma.

They step onto the tar-paper roof, cross over to a low brick wall, and hoist themselves up onto the ledge, the street sixty feet below. The entire city is laid out before them, a mass of light divided into three pie pieces by the blackness of the rivers. Everything is lit from below by the streetlights, the buildings shown in stark relief on their sides and dark on their roofs, so that it looks as though someone is shining a dirty yellow flashlight up from below. Packs of students from the university roam up and down Forbes, but up on the roof they are removed from the shouts and laughter, the sounds of traffic and car horns barely touching them. They sit on the ledge awhile, hovering over the glow of yellowed light like gods.

34

The night before we went in, they gathered us in the planning tent around a steel table covered with maps and satellite images and lists of coordinates and frequencies.

They told us this was probably the most hostile village in the entire fucking region. They had found them, they said. They were ninety-nine percent certain. These were the guys who had killed Jacobs. Probably Marin, too. Finally, we had them. They were in this village.

"*Light 'em up,*" *they said. But they didn't know what they were saying.*

They estimated that, after we took the boats up the river, it would take us an hour to hike our way across the plain and over to the rise, two klicks west of the village.

They would be coming in hard, and they wanted to know whether anyone in the village suspected. Observe and report, they said. Radio in anything weird, anything out of the ordinary, they said. And now, in hindsight, I think it's odd that no one questioned it. No one asked how we were supposed to know, after being there for only a few hours, what was weird and out of the ordinary and what wasn't, what was totally normal.

They told us that when the time came, we would go in with the rest.

"What if we run into contacts?" asked Skeets.

"Assume hostility," they said.

"If we're spotted?" I'm not sure, but I think it was Dom who asked this.

"Light 'em up," they said.

It was a phrase we used a lot, and it was said easily, almost casually. But what I think now, what I did not realize at the time, is that for all the people gathered around that table, for all of the planning, and the training, and the money spent on equipment, for all the time that we all spent out there, there wasn't a soul involved who thought about it long enough to know exactly what that meant.

35

"What's that noise?" asks Hakma, and then Jonas hears it, too, the static-click-static of sideband radios, and they rush over to the building's adjacent side, and look over the edge in time to see two men in blue uniforms enter through the same door they did.

"Police," says Jonas, his mind racing. "Just act like you live here." Their plan set, Jonas is surprised to find himself relatively unconcerned as they stand on the roof, waiting, and pleased to find that if he concentrates in just the right way, he can keep the metal door through which the policemen will shortly emerge from drifting out of his field of vision.

"Hi, there, officers," says Hakma, smiling as the policemen come out through the door and onto the roof.

"Hi," says the one in front, a short, balding man who looks to be at least fifty. "What are you doing up here?"

"Oh, just looking at the city," says Jonas.

"Do you live here?"

"Yes, sir."

"Which apartment?"

"Number six, sir."

"Uh-huh. Can I see some identification?"

"Sure."

"Uh-huh. Now, it says here that you live over on Calvert."

"Right. I am actually just here visiting."

"But you said you lived here."

"Well, right, but when you said 'you,' I thought you meant the collective 'you,' not just me. See, you're supposed to designate, if you're talking to a group."

"Uh-huh. And how about you," says the officer, looking hard at Hakma. "And this time, just so there's no confusion, I mean the singular 'you,' as opposed to the collective. Do *you* live here?"

"Well . . ." says Hakma.

Later, as he sits on the cold steel bench in the holding cell at the police station, Jonas will recall how some things seem so clear when you first see them, clouded though your mind may be by fear or alcohol, but when you see them again later, in hindsight, the foolishness of that initial clarity becomes obvious. But the foolishness of what he is about to do is not at all obvious to him at this point. The point at which Hakma is trying to explain his ID situation. The point at which Jonas decides to run.

Too late, he realizes that he has been paying so much attention to the policeman in front of him, the short, bald, out-of-shape-looking man doing all the talking, that he barely notices the policeman behind. In fact, he doesn't really notice him at all until he is trying to run past him, and in one swift motion he kicks Jonas's leg out from under him, and Jonas falls onto the tar-paper roof.

The policeman, who has until now not said a word, bends over Jonas where he has fallen, and finally speaks.

He says, "You're under arrest."

CONFESSION

He hears the voice of his savior. It is gentle, and deep, and touched by the lilting music of the Pennsylvania hills.

It is also incoherent. Long strings of muttered words seem to float in the air between them, and Younis has trouble putting them into context.

"Maybe you knew her."

"Knew who?"

"That kid. Was not supposed to go that way."

"Which way?"

"Except that it was."

"Was what?"

"It was designed to happen that way."

The discussion has spun out over the course of an hour, circling and doubling back upon itself, and Younis can find no firm footing in the midst of it. So he sits back and allows the words to dance around him.

"Maybe the south. Maybe the east would have been better. Choppers. We should have used choppers. Skeets was saying that. Should have landed us right there. But the river. First mistake. The goddamned river! Whose Rambo idea was that? Stupid. Poor planning."

The words swirl around him, and at some point, Younis becomes aware that Christopher is looking at him, waiting for a response.

"Do you know what I mean?" says Christopher.

"Sir, I honestly have no idea what you are talking about," says Younis.

Christopher takes a breath. He focuses his attention, and then finally speaks in full and coherent sentences.

"When you do something like what we did, down there in the valley, once you make the decision to do it, it takes on a life of its own. They always tell you that the most important thing is to not make any mistakes. But sometimes, the decision to do it in the first place is the mistake."

Younis doesn't say anything, and turns away from Christopher's stare and looks into the fire.

"Look," says Christopher, pulling the leather journal out of his pack, untying the tie, opening it, and handing it to Younis. "Maybe you should read this."

We called her Jezebel, and she was not supposed to be there.

She just appeared. One second there was nothing, just the open field. Then she was there, walking toward us. I hoped that maybe she was a mirage.

We picked that spot, just below the ridge, because it was perfect. It was two kilometers west of the village. It was on a little rise. We came up the river, arrived that morning, and dug our position just as the sky was getting lighter in the dawn. We had our firing sectors laid out, and had everything covered between us and the village.

Then we sat and waited.

Jezebel appeared late in the afternoon.

We had already been ambushed so many times. We had lost three guys. Jacobs had gone down two days before. Some of them wanted payback. We knew they had a house in the village; we knew they used that road. We knew everything we needed to know.

Skeets called her out first. She was about a hundred meters out and wandering in our general direction. How old could she have been? Eight? Younger? Her head was uncovered, and she wore a long white dress that billowed behind her as she walked. In the sun her dark arms and hair stood out against the whiteness. Every few steps, she would stop and look at the ground, and bend down and pick something up, a stone or something, and roll it around in the palm of her hand. Then she would either throw it off to the side, if it didn't meet her mysterious criteria, or she would tuck it into a little cloth bag she wore over her shoulder.

"Vehicles on the road," *said Skeets. He was looking through the scope, moving his cheek against the gunstock.* "Heading toward us."

We had been briefed. We had been told these were the guys who killed Jacobs. We were reminded of the lack of hard intel, the preciousness of knowledge, the uniqueness of this opportunity. The weight of it pushed down on our shoulders. None of us had slept in thirty-six hours.

And then she was a hundred meters out, directly between us and the village. She bent down again to look at another stone, picked it up, this one meeting her requirements, and she filed it away into her bag. On the road behind her, two white Subarus kicked up the dust.

She was not supposed to be there.

Skeets said, "Gimme the word, sir." *His voice sounded strained.*

Now she was less than fifty meters from us. She stood up in the field and looked around, off into the distance. I wished she would turn around and walk back to the village. I prayed that I would close my eyes and then open them, and that she would be gone. Instead, she stood for a long time in that no-man's-land between us and the village, as though lost in thought. Then she turned and looked directly at us. She smiled, like she had just glimpsed the exact stone she had been out there looking for that whole time, the one she was looking for, the right size and shape and color, the stone she most wanted in her little canvas sack.

She walked straight toward us.

"Incoming," Skeets said, looking at the road. "We need the order, Chris."

I looked down at him and saw that his trigger hand was shaking, almost imperceptibly, and that he was breathing too fast.

In my mind, I put her odds at about fifty-fifty.

3

Jail is not what Jonas expects. Metal bars do not confine him; food is not some sort of gray slop served on a steel tray. In fact, he's there only for the night, so no food is served at all. He empties his pockets into a wire basket, which is carried nonchalantly away by an obese, uniformed man with a large mole on his cheek. He is allowed to make one phone call before being led into a white room with a heavy door and two long steel benches bolted to opposite walls. Actually, he gathers, it is called a holding cell, which makes it sound almost maternal. The walls are white with dark scuff marks, as though someone wearing black-soled shoes has stutter-stepped across them. Someone has etched the word "smoot" into one wall with a sharp object, the letters sliced thinly into the chipped paint, and a dark splotch stains one corner of the shiny concrete floor. He's just in for the night, he is told again, for his own good, so he can sleep it off. But someone will have to come down and sign him out in the morning.

Other than the steel benches, the room is empty, spinning a little in his vision, filled with only the memory of former residents, the marked-up walls implying carelessness and
violence.

"Slow night," says the guard.

For a time he sits on the steel bench and stares at the back
of the door. He notices that something is written there, roughly
printed at an angle in small, pale letters, written using a blue
marker evidently down to its last gasp of ink. Unable to read
it from where he is seated, he crosses the room to get a better
look. It says, "Jezus died for you're sinz."

Jonas goes back and sits down. The bench is just wide
enough to lie down upon, which he does, his head against the
hard steel and already starting to ache, and he falls asleep.

4

Rose gathers them together in ones and twos, writing letters
and making phone calls, and even, occasionally, despite her
unfamiliarity with technology, sending an e-mail. She will
act as a facilitator. When they meet her, they will usually be
impressed by how big she seems, her personality filling the
room, this little woman with the shock of red hair and the
booming voice, and the hugs she gives out like Halloween
candy.

She is deft in her ability to not allow the conversation

to come around to her own loss. It is not about her, she always says, even though they know that, at least to some degree, it is.

5

He remembers that they came to see him while he was still in the hospital. When they asked him whether he wanted to come to America, he was surprised. He would have to think about it, he said. And he did. He thought about it for days.

He does not remember making the decision. For a moment after he told them yes, he thought that maybe there was a disconnection between his brain and his mouth. He didn't remember actually making the decision, only the act of telling them about it, and he remembers being a little surprised to hear himself saying it. He pictured his mouth making the decision, and the thought made him smile almost imperceptibly, an expression mistaken, at the time, for happiness.

He thinks about it often. Two words, "I'll go," that mark the difference between two paths, two entirely different lives. Words that set in motion a chain of events stretching to fill years. Sometimes he wonders what it would have been like had he said no, as he almost did, balancing on that sharp edge of time in the moment before he opened his mouth, that split second that grows in his mind, stretching as surely as the subsequent events to fill another, different lifetime. Perhaps he'd still be back there, a refugee and not part of a diaspora. Perhaps he'd be dead, left to starve in the street, or left to sell himself, or sell others, or steal and kill.

Or maybe not. Maybe it all would have turned out the same, but by different means. Maybe it all would have happened, the plane ride, the suburban adolescence, the university, Shakri, everything, right up until he was where he found himself right then, as he thought about it, in his present reality, sitting on a steel bench in a jail cell, somewhere in western Pennsylvania.

6

Thursday, October 14 (AP)—U.S. military officials today acknowledged a raid that occurred last week and claimed the lives of two American soldiers. A third U.S. soldier is listed as missing in action. Army spokeswoman Emily C. Walters declined to identify the soldiers pending notification of their families.

One official, who spoke on condition of anonymity, said that the early-morning raid had resulted in the killing of twelve suspected high-level insurgent fighters and the capture of ten others.

Details of the raid were not yet available. Officials estimate that an additional ten to fifteen civilians may also have been killed or injured during the fighting.

The area in which the raid occurred has been described as a lawless border region and a source of consternation to U.S.

military officials because of the insurgents' ability to blend in with the local population and the relative absence of national governing structures.

7

Out of the corner of my eye, I saw her go down. I don't know who shot her. Everybody was popping off like crazy. We were shooting. They were shooting. We were trying to knock out their vehicles before they made it into the village. But we didn't even manage to succeed at that.

I don't know who hit her. I'm pretty sure it was one of ours. Funny thing is, it didn't even look violent. She just fell over. I remember her hair puffed out a little, right before she went down, but that might be my imagination. I don't think I misremember it, though. Not something like that.

It was nothing, really. A blip. At the time. Nothing. For a while, I thought she was going to make it. I thought maybe she had simply had the good sense to get out of the way. It happened so fast. She just fell down. Like she was tired. Like she wanted to take a nap.

8

Like his past, Jonas's future comes to him as a series of images, half dreams that flicker, one to another, as though lit by a strobe. In one, he is married, a hazy female form who may or may not be Shakri, and a child tugs at his pant leg. Then he is walking down a path through the woods, when suddenly he is blocked by a precipitous gorge. Then he is being awarded some kind of prize, or medal, on a podium above a cheering throng. Then he walks down a street in a large city, car horns blaring and a sheen of dirt on his skin. He must cross the canyon, but no obvious method presents itself. He is carried over the heads of the crowd, his name (which name?) chanted as he floats on a tide of hands. A tree has fallen across the gorge, and looks to be a way across. He climbs onto the fallen log and takes a step forward. A wooden ladder appears in the middle of the street, fixed to the ground and stretching so high that he cannot see the top of it, which disappears into clouds above the tall buildings. He is halfway across the fallen tree when he looks down. He grasps the ladder and places his foot on the first rung. Halfway up the ladder he can no longer see the ground. Neither, standing on the fallen tree, can he see the bottom of the chasm. He looks out to see that he is balanced on the rim of a pint glass, beer lapping at its edge like a frothy, golden sea. Vertigo overcomes him, and he cannot take another step. He imagines falling backward into the glass, cleansing himself in it, the pleasant numbing sensation in his limbs and the bubbles tickling his skin. He feels the heady, airy feeling of knowing he could fall, the release of doing so. But although he could do so at any moment, he has not yet fallen. So there he stands, hovering over everything, unable to fall and unable to cross, unable to make the decision to do either.

9

Sometimes Younis wakes on the mountain to a scratching sound. At first, still asleep, he thinks it's a rat clawing at the earth beside his head, searching for morsels. But then, alert, he realizes that it is the sound of pencil on paper. Outside, the wind whistles up the slope past the cave's shallow mouth, and he is surprised he can hear anything above it. But the scratching sound is distinctive, sandpapering his consciousness, dotted by sharp points of punctuation. Younis keeps his eyes closed, listens as the scratching sound fills the cave. Then he opens one eye, just enough to see. Across the fire, Christopher's attention seems entirely occupied by the page before him.

Another time, Younis wakes to a different scratching, this time a longer and sharper sound with a pronounced metallic ring at the end of it, and he looks up to see Christopher hunched next to the fire, a whetstone balanced in one hand, moving his other hand back and forth from the wrist, the long blade of his combat knife flashing occasionally in the flickering light.

Younis notices that when Christopher sharpens his knife, he sits facing him across the fire, the book lying shut next to him on the ground with the pencil tucked inside. But when Christopher writes in his book, everything is reversed. He sits facing away from Younis, the knife either lying on the ground beside him or stuck, hilt up, in the rocky ground.

Younis finds being woken by either of these sounds unnerving. Both actions, the sharpening of the knife and the writing in the book, are obsessive. At one point, Christopher sees that Younis is awake, stops what he is doing, looks over with a half smile, and offers him something to drink, asks about his pain, tells him he has only one dose of morphine remaining.

Younis begins to wonder what is going on. Having arrived, having set up camp, Christopher seems inclined to stay forever. Younis tries to determine how long they have been on the mountain, he drifting in and out of consciousness, Christopher scratching out his defenses. He wonders why Christopher seems so unconcerned about getting back to his unit. He wonders why he has made no effort to get in touch with his comrades. He wonders why Christopher seems not to care whether they ever leave.

And the more he ponders these questions, the less he likes any of the answers he can find.

10

A photograph: Three soldiers stand tall in rising dust that has probably been kicked up by a helicopter's rotor wash. They are covered in Kevlar and strapped with equipment, and they wear dark sunglasses that make them unknowable, showing only their stern mouths. They carry their weapons pointed at the ground, and behind them sits a pile of boxes and large bundles covered by a tightly wrapped tarpaulin. They are waiting for something. Something important, something urgent. They are invincible, human only in the way that robots look human, as if they have been created to look that way, and could easily have been created to look another way if that had suited the purpose of their creator.

Another soldier, a local soldier, sits on a crate in the dust beside them. If the standing soldiers are approximately human, this soldier sitting in the dust is entirely so. He does not wear sunglasses or Kevlar or a stern mouth. He wears a mustache, and his helmet looks to be fifty years old. His face shows clearly under the helmet's broad brim, the bags under his eyes, the wrinkles on his face, and he looks to be wiping from his brow an accumulation of dust and sweat. He seems to be tired. So tired. He seems to just want this whole thing to be over.

II

Rose does not need to raise her voice very much in order to be heard over the murmur of conversation that fills the recreation center. Her distinctive contralto reverberates from the steel folding chairs, the laminated tabletops, the worn Formica tiles, all of it lit from above by hanging fluorescent tubes. She tells those assembled that Pastor McConnell will lead a prayer group later in the afternoon, or that the most recent funding drive has raised a significant amount, or that she has received a letter from Senator So-and-so.

Some of them are already turning gray at their temples, she thinks. Some are losing their hair, like cancer patients. Some are talking continuously, as though trying to expel pent-up emotion in controlled bursts, while others remain mostly silent. A few seem to be totally unaffected.

She will gather them together, first at the church near her home in the Pennsylvania hills, then regionally, renting out moderately sized meeting halls for the occasion, then nationally, in convention centers, as the need for the organization grows in direct proportion to the nation's grief.

She is careful not to talk much about herself at these meetings. If forced, she says only that she has lost her son, biting her lower lip, nodding her head slightly, commiserating fully with someone else she knows has lost at least that much. She feels no need to talk about it, does not want to burden others with her story, but gains strength from their presence, from being connected to them.

Some of the meetings take on an Irish-wake quality, boisterous and laughing back tears. Others are somber. They share in common an underlying stream of activism, of information sharing, of tips about veterans' benefits and job training and education funding, and a subtle segregation between the veterans themselves and those who love them, the former finding one another out and talking in slightly rougher language and at lower registers.

And they also share the events' organizer, a little woman with red hair and a booming voice who calls them together for a moment of silence, or an item of housekeeping, or just to tell them that dinner is being served in the dining hall.

12

He remembers waking up in the firelight. He remembers the dull ache covering the length of his arm. He remembers coughing on woodsmoke. He remembers his legs tingling and numb. He remembers the pain sharpening as he came to. He remembers the figure hunched on the other side of the fire. He remembers hearing one of two noises: the metallic ring of steel on a whetstone, or the rough scratch of pencil on paper. He remembers not knowing which of the two noises he preferred.

13

She was not supposed to be there.

She appeared, gently, across the dusty field. She was not a mirage. We were dug in where we were supposed to be, just like we were supposed to be, two kilometers to the west of the village. But there she was. Poor planning.

Skeets called it out first. "Two hundred meters," he said.

She was rolling a stone around in the palm of her hand. Then she was walking toward us, her long white dress billowing behind her as she walked, reflecting the sun. Then the trucks were on the road, kicking up dust. Then she bent down again and picked up another stone, which she threw off to the side with a laugh.

And then she was a hundred meters out. And then she was fifty. She was not supposed to be there.

I wished she would turn around and walk back to the village, prayed that I would close my eyes and then open them, and that she would be gone. Instead, she smiled and walked straight toward us.

"I need the order, Chris," whispered Skeets.

I saw that his trigger hand was shaking, almost imperceptibly, and that he was breathing too fast, taking in great gulps of air.

It didn't matter, though.

"Light 'em up," I said.

"Should we not go?" says Younis again.

But Christopher is not paying attention. He appears unaware that Younis has said anything, or even that he is present. His lips are firmly shut, his eyes squinting in concentration as his hand moves, laboring obsessively.

"Hey!" says Younis.

Christopher looks up, reluctantly, to meet Younis's gaze with blank incomprehension.

"Should we not leave?" Younis says.

"We cannot leave. There is too much to do here."

Younis is amazed by the fact that even while he speaks, even while he is not looking, his hand continues to move, carrying on with its work.

"What, never?" says Younis.

Christopher only continues to stare blankly, and then he winces in unmistakable pain. For a moment, Younis thinks that maybe the question somehow stung him. But then he looks down to see that Christopher has pricked his thumb, and that his pant leg is stained with tiny drops. He quickly grabs some gauze from his pack and wraps it around the thumb.

"Ah, well," he says, once the wound is stanched. "What's a little blood, shed in the common defense?"

15

There is no knock at the door, no buzzer sounding warning; no one asks permission to enter. The holding-cell door simply opens and there is Paul. He wears a rumpled T-shirt underneath a plaid, unbuttoned flannel, and his hair is uncombed.

"You're only the second client I've ever had to visit in jail," he says. "The first one burned down her house. What did you do?"

Jonas sits up and rubs his head. "Nothing," he says, breathing out.

Paul's expression tightens, his lips pursing together, and he turns to leave, saying, "Well, then you can get yourself out."

"No, wait," says Jonas. "I, Hakma, we went into this building up on Fifth, to see the view. They say I was trespassing. Intoxicated publicly. Although we weren't in public, really."

"Where's your friend?"

"I don't know."

"He's not here. But you are, Jonas."

"I tried to run."

Before they are even out of the police station, Paul spells out two conditions that Jonas must meet. They are nonnegotiable if Paul is to continue working with him. If he doesn't oblige, Paul says, he'll wish Jonas all the best and be on his way. The choice is his.

Jonas says that it's all just pointless, that he is unable to comprehend why Paul stands by him. "I'm not worth it," he says. But then, reluctantly, he agrees.

The next evening, Jonas sits to one side of a small circle of people facing one another across a linoleum-floored basement. He knows that he is supposed to say something. He has been listening to them for ten minutes, going around the circle one after another, all saying the same thing. Some of them say it quietly; some share it with voices full of pride, some as though they have just run a great distance.

"Hello, my name is Jonas," he says, and the words come out as they're supposed to, but he thinks it is all ridiculous, stupid. He can barely keep a straight face. He pictures everyone he has ever known laughing at him. It's all so pathetic. But he goes, because he has agreed, and because he knows that several of Paul's other clients are in the group, and that they will tell Paul if he does not.

After the first meeting he says to Paul that it's okay, that he doesn't think he needs to go, tells him he's not that far gone, doesn't really have a problem, tells him it doesn't mean anything to him.

Paul assures Jonas that he does not care.

"It's been one day since my last drink."

"Just keep going," says Paul. "That's the deal."

At the meetings, Jonas always sits in a chair by the door, figuring that from there he can get out quickly if he has to.

16

"Maybe you can tell me what happened the night you left your village," says Paul. "Or maybe you can talk about what happened between then and the time you were found, up in the hills, and taken to the hospital."

Jonas believes himself to be physically incapable of talking about it any further. He feels his stomach clench into a tight ball, his jaw stiffen. There are things Jonas will not talk about. He has developed a skill for deflecting the conversation if it appears to be approaching any of them. He stares at the floor, wishing the moment would go away, vowing to stay silent until it does.

"What else happened, Jonas?"

Almost involuntarily, Jonas tilts his head to the side, as though someone has grabbed the back of his neck and is pinching the muscles together. He feels his face contort slightly, squinting his eye and grimacing his cheek. Once or twice, he opens his mouth to say something, but nothing escapes. The silence drags on, forcing the air from the room.

"What else?" says Paul.

"He saved my life," says Jonas finally, a bare whisper that catches in his throat.

17

Jezebel laid out in that field all day. It was a standoff. Seemed like every person who lived in that village was armed and holed up inside it. They wouldn't come out, so we had to wait for the firepower to go in. And she laid out there in no-man's-land.

She was about forty meters away, and I found that if I set my mind in the right way, I could convince myself that she had simply gotten tired and put her head down for a nap. I could pretend she was going to pop up any minute, awake and refreshed, and laugh her way back home.

I don't know who started calling her Jezebel. We were lying in the dugout, and someone, maybe it was Gordy, nodded his head and whispered, "I'm so tired I could sleep like Jezebel over there." And then someone chuckled. And then we all called her that. She became our mascot. Recon team Jezebel.

Maybe I shouldn't have, but I felt responsible. When the moon came up, I went out to get her. It was this weird crescent moon that seemed to give off more light than it should have. I walked out toward her, and the silver moonlight shone off the rocks and her dress with the same intensity, so that I kept losing sight of her among the field of stones. When I got to her, I bent down to look her over. I couldn't find a wound anywhere. For a second I thought that maybe she really was asleep. Her eyes were closed and she looked peaceful, at rest. Then I saw a tiny, dark dot on her throat. Only *when I picked her up I realized there was nothing left to the back of her neck.*

I lifted her and carried her as gently as I could back up to our position. The order had come down that we were going to go in, so they were all folding up their kits, hoisting their packs to their shoulders. Turner hacked at the bottom of the shallow dugout with his folding spade to make it deep enough. Probably we shouldn't have, but it felt proper. I stepped down into the pit and placed Jezebel as easily as I could on the floor of it. I put a rock under her head to prop her up a little, but that didn't look very comfortable, so I pulled out my green handkerchief and folded it under her head.

We pushed the dry earth on top of her. Someone whispered that prayer, the one about ashes and dust, because that's all anyone could think of. None of us could remember the whole thing properly, so we mumbled some words to tell her how sorry we were that it had to go the way it did. And then they all filed off, down the ridge, getting ready to go in.

But I stayed there a few minutes, staring at the earth. Something caught my eye in the moonlight, a little flash on the ground, and I bent down and picked up a gray stone with a streak of white quartz in it that reflected the moon.

I still have that stone, here in my pocket. Probably it is not one of the stones Jezebel collected in her little bag that morning, and probably it didn't fall out as we buried her.

But sometimes I pretend that it did.

18

"Maybe we can try something," says Paul. "Something to help you explore this a little more, talk about the rest of it."

They have been sitting for twenty minutes in silence. Jonas feels pinned to his chair like an insect.

"I already have," he says.

"But there's more to it, isn't there?"

Jonas says nothing.

"Isn't there," says Paul again.

"Well, then, maybe you can tell me," says Jonas at last, "because I can't say."

"Okay," says Paul, "if you don't know, maybe you can guess. Sitting here looking at the floor is not going to cut it. Picture yourself up there on the mountain. What's going on? What's there? What do you see? What do you hear? Lots of things might have happened. Maybe you can tell me about those things. Maybe you can tell me what might have happened. Hypothetically."

"I don't know that I can."

"Try."

19

Jonas tells Paul the same thing he told Rose Henderson while he sat in her living room, drinking juice and eating cookies.

A possibility, says Jonas. He says that maybe he left his village. Maybe he was compelled. Maybe he was forced to leave by events upon which he refused to dwell. Maybe he found himself all alone, up on the mountain, huddled in the mouth of the cave his father had told him about months earlier. Maybe he was unable, for a variety of reasons, to decide between living and dying.

And maybe at that moment, Christopher stepped onto the side of the mountain as though descending from a cloud, and built him a fire, and warmed him, and fed him, and stitched him up, and eased his pain. And then, his work done, maybe Christopher stepped back into the void, dissolved back into the air like a thought.

20

Rose runs into them sometimes, usually at a regional meeting, or a national one, because they are spread out across the country. They always seem to already know who she is, and they approach, tentatively, to introduce themselves. I knew

Christopher, they say, and they surround her like a cordon, off to one side of the room, all of them nearly twice her height, and they tell her about her son.

Early on, they tell her, he developed a reputation for being the calm one, the quiet one, the deep one. In the chaos of basic training, the dirty jokes about girls and would-be girl-friends, the rowdy towel-snapping and the occasional fistfights, Christopher always maintained a mellow, almost aloof pres-ence. Even as a noob (a newbie, they explain, as they all were at one time), he seemed to know the score better even than the gunnery sergeant. He suffered the yelling, the physical training, the hazing, with an air of detachment, as though he were watching street theater.

One of them tells her a story, not meant to alarm, he assures her, but this is what Christopher was like.

There was once a mistake made during a live-fire exercise, and a grenade went off much too close to their dugout position, showering them with dirt. In the absolute silence following the explosion, they took a hasty roll call, tallying the living, all present and accounted for, until they came to his name, and there was silence.

"Henderson," they say. "Henderson." They look around.

And when he finally answers, his voice is like the open wind, entirely unconcerned, and possibly even a little annoyed at being compelled to speak. There they were, all freaking out, and then there's this voice.

"Yeah, man," said the voice. "I'm fine." Yeah, man, just like that. And they smile at the memory.

Rose seems happy to meet them, talk to them, seems

touched even by their fumbling efforts to comfort her, and in her desire to not dwell on her own loss, her desire to accommodate them, she refrains from pointing out the irony of hearing from them about the first time, the time when her son came back.

21

Jonas blacks out. He wakes up in a boat, tied to a tree, floating in the shallows of the river, down by the Fourteenth Street bridge. Another time, he wakes up with a shout when a cigarette burns his chest, having fallen from his mouth as he nodded off. He wakes up in someone's living room, the floor covered with people who have not yet woken. He wakes up in front of his television set, his pants bunched around his ankles. He wakes up to a dog licking his face. He wakes up next to nameless girls. He wakes to find himself covered with incomprehensible bruises. He wakes up choking on vomit. He wakes up and has no idea where he is. He wakes up to laughter, still sitting in a booth at the bar, and everyone turned to smile at him, the bright strobe of a camera flash, and it's not until he gets home, stumbles into the bathroom, and looks in the mirror that he realizes that on his face has been drawn the face of a clown.

22

In another photo, a group of soldiers dressed in sand-colored camouflage and weighed down by gear crouch beside a low wall. The sky is overcast, and all of them except one have removed their large, dark sunglasses, which lie strapped on top of their helmets. Behind them, farther down the wall, in the background, a goat stands unconcerned in the dust.

Each of the soldiers looks in a different direction, as though they are each either keeping watch over a different quadrant or have no idea in which direction they should be looking. The soldier in the foreground grips his weapon so tightly that his fingers have turned white at the knuckles. Because they have removed their sunglasses from their faces (all of them except one), their expressions are clearly visible. They look to be on the verge of panic.

23

The sun setting again on the mountain, Younis feels himself caught in a whirlpool.

One moment he fears for his life. He has seen it in Christopher's eyes. He has snapped. He peers from across the fire through a suspicious mask, eyes narrowed to dark slits, glances filled with menace. Younis fears he will not live through the night. He wonders only why it has not been done already.

The next moment he fills with rage. He barely cares whether he lives. For what is his heart now but a hole, what is his life but loss, what is the sum of his entire being but absence? And who is to blame for that?

And the next moment he thinks that maybe they will go their separate ways in peace. After all, one of them saved the other's life. That must count for something. He almost trusts him. They are victims of circumstance, and his own misfortune is theirs shared.

He tries to settle on one interpretation. He searches for an objective reality. He struggles in vain to slow the wheel of conviction spinning uncontrollably in his mind. The more he tries to get a fix on the truth, the more he is dragged in circles, unable to see clearly, unable to stop.

24

At first, Jonas thinks the letter on university stationery is an invitation to another student-faculty function. He opens it expecting to be asked to a reception or a dinner. He is pleased by this, thinks that maybe it's what he needs, a little social interaction with people other than his regular circle. Feeling for some reason that an invitation should be opened properly, rather than simply torn, he goes to the kitchen drawer and, unable to locate a letter opener, pulls out a sharp knife.

Office of the Dean of Students

University of Pittsburgh
1275 Forbes Avenue
Pittsburgh, PA 15601

We regret to inform you that it has become necessary to place you on academic suspension. You are welcome to apply for readmission to the university following a one-semester absence, during which time you will be required to enroll in remedial classes. Below, you will find information about the remedial classes offered by the university and the procedures for enrolling. Please note that achieving passing grades in these classes is merely a prerequisite for readmission, and they do not in and of themselves convey academic credit.

If you choose not to enroll in these remedial classes, you will be permanently suspended at the end of the next term. You will then be unable to attend the university for a period of three years, after which time you may reapply, and will be given the same status and consideration as any newly applying student.

It is also strongly recommended that you seek emotional and/or academic counseling, if you are not doing so already. It has been found that students who are unable to progress satisfactorily with their academic requirements are often affected by underlying personal problems, and that by sorting through these issues it is possible to make a successful return to academic standing. *Enclosed please find information about some of the mental health services available, both through the university and in the larger community.*

We wish you the best of luck for your continued progress and development. Please do not hesitate to contact our office with any questions you may have concerning this action.

Very best regards,
Roger Mineras
Dean of Students

25

We had orders.

We had orders. We had orders. We had orders. We had orders. We had orders. We had orders. We had orders. We had orders. We had orders.

Those were the guys, they said. Light 'em up.

An order is an order. We could not risk letting them go. I'm sorry it had to go the way it did. I really am. I would change it in an instant if I could. I would go back in time and do it differently. I would ask questions. I would raise objections. I would ask to see the intel. I would pay attention to the nagging sensation in the core of my brain that was trying to tell me that something was wrong. Truly I would.

But we had orders, and they were very clear.
An order is an order.
We had orders.

26

"Hello, my name is Jonas, and I may have a problem. You know. With drinking, I guess."

"Hello, Jonas."

"And, Jonas, how long has it been since you've had a drink?"

"About an hour and a half."

27

In this photo is Christopher, wearing the same uniform, same gun, but he does not wear the dark sunglasses and therefore it is easy to tell that it is him. He looks young. He seems to hold his weapon's weight with difficulty. His body is turned slightly to the right as he walks through the dust, and he looks in the general direction of the camera, but off to the side and down, as though assessing something on the ground to the photographer's right. His expression is determined, but slightly unsure, an expression which strives to betray nothing even as it betrays everything, the expression of a young boy playing poker with grown men.

Behind him, slightly blurred, is a house or mound or hill, some large object, but it is impossible to tell exactly what it is, because it is covered with people sitting, as though in an arena, watching the soldier who has suddenly appeared among them. These people, all of them men, wear beards. Some of them wear tightly wound cloth *lugees* wrapped around their heads, while some of them are bareheaded. To the right side of the picture, in the background, two of these men appear to be talking, whispering. They look to be amused, as though they are quietly making a wager.

28

He has had a recurring thought. A daydream. He tells it to Hakma over drinks.

They have contacted him. He walks down the fluorescent corridor. Travelers rush past him pulling wheeled suitcases or hunched under weighty backpacks. He carries no bag, nothing to hold him up at security, which he has eased through like a leaf floating through rapids. He knows what he is supposed to do. A young woman hurries ahead of him, gripping her child's hand.

"Come on," she says to the unconcerned boy. "They're already boarding."

He steps onto the swift conveyor, adjusting his balance as the belt takes over. He is being pulled along now, set in motion, no longer entirely under his own power.

He doesn't know how they found him, how they knew he was ready.

He finds the bathroom, the one at the far end of the long corridor, the least-used. He waits for everyone to leave, for the bathroom to be empty, a lull. Then he goes over to the trash can, which is stainless steel and set into the wall. He reaches into it, rummages through damp paper towels until his hand strikes something solid, a strap, which he grabs and pulls. It is heavier than he imagined, and he struggles to pull it out of the trash.

He knows what to do.

He hauls it into a stall, locks the door, removes his jacket and shirt, lowers the vest over his shoulders, straps it around his body, heavy as the earth. Then he puts his clothes back on over it.

A voice, commanding and feminine, echoing from the tiled walls, urges him to report unattended baggage. He opens the stall door to see that the bathroom has filled with people, and he is momentarily confused, unable to find the exit. When at last he does, he joins the throng of travelers, of fathers and mothers and aunts and brothers struggling under the weight of luggage and worry, or buoyed by excitement and anticipation, or driven by determined focus, but he feels no connection to any of them, because he is already gone.

29

I thought she might make it. I really did.

I keep replaying it in my mind.

I must have been delusional. I thought something could still happen after the shooting started. I thought there would be a little break, then, a space of time during which she would trip and fall out of the way, or hear her mother calling, or turn around and get out of there at the last moment. She could have bent down to pick up another rock. I don't know, anything. Run light-speed across the field, back to where she came from.

Even now, in my mind, I want to yell at her to get down.

But there was no space of time, no gap. It was instant. I spoke and the guns roared. They continue to roar. I cannot get them out of my head.

She was standing there, curious and vibrant, and then she was a crumpled sack of laundry on the rocks. There was no time for anything, no gust of wind that would blow the bullets off course, no time for angels to descend from the sky and lift her off to safety.

30

Maybe, he tells Paul. Maybe he fled his village, was forced to leave. Maybe he found his way up to the cave his father had told him about. Maybe Christopher saved his life, stitched him up, built him a fire.

But then maybe at some point Christopher started to lose it. Maybe he was crazy. Maybe he thought they needed to move, or realized that they were in the wrong place; maybe he thought they needed to be somewhere else. Maybe he started freaking out because he suddenly realized that he was AWOL on some mountaintop with a wounded hajji.

Maybe Christopher insisted that they pack up, move out. Maybe they rushed to get to the top of some other hill, that hill over there, the one on top of which Christopher suddenly realized they were supposed to be. But maybe, when they got up on top of that one, Christopher realized that it was not the right hill either. Maybe he looked at a map. Maybe this happened a few times. Maybe they were tired. Maybe Christopher started thinking they were supposed to be in a valley, rather than on a mountaintop. That valley over there, and maybe they wandered all over the southern mountains, wandered for days.

Maybe one time it started getting dark while they were out searching around. Maybe the path was difficult, lined with boulders and rocks that were just the right size to trip over, and maybe they were tired. Maybe the trail was narrow, and the mountainside fell away next to it, off into the darkness. Maybe Christopher stepped the wrong way, caught a rock with the side of his boot and tripped, stumbled, fell over the cliff edge. Maybe one instant he was there, and the next he was not. Maybe he dropped without making a sound, silently, like a stone.

31

They tell Rose that he was selfless, that he was always the first to help out. If a noob packed too much gear and struggled over the hills they'd been climbing all morning, it was always Christopher who offered to switch packs with him, carry for him his extra weight. He never seemed to mind cleaning the latrine, or pulling zero-hour guard duty, both of which, he said, gave him time to think. Through anything that came his way, he maintained a Zen-like aura of impregnability. Someone started to call him Yoda, a nickname created in an effort to get to the heart of his calm bearing, and it stuck for a while, but always felt insufficient, cartoony.

One of them, the son of a religious family from Oregon, tells her that he always went to Christopher for advice. His family told him that he should talk only to the chaplain, and he did that sometimes, too, but he always found Christopher to be more real, wise in the same way the chaplain was wise, but street-smart in a way that the chaplain was not.

They tell her they had total confidence in him, both as a soldier and as a person. They tell her he gave them strength. They tell her she could be proud of him, that he was a real credit to her as a mother. They tell her that anyone should be proud beyond words to have had a son like him.

32

He sees two versions of the future. Paul asks him to describe them. One is shadowed, and the other is lit by truth.

"I don't know what to do," says Jonas.

"Do?" says Paul. "You know what you have to do."

"No, I don't."

"Sure you do. You have to start making good choices. You have to establish a track record of positive action."

Jonas looks at the silver statue on Paul's desk, molded into its indescribable shape, like an ellipse, or the melting clocks he once saw in a painting.

"I don't know," says Jonas. "I feel like I'm running out of time."

33

In the foreground, two soldiers, one of them lying prone on the ground, looking down the sight of a sniper rifle supported by a tripod on the earth in front of him. The other soldier crouches beside him, scanning the horizon, a mortar tube slung around his back and the butt of his rifle lodged into his shoulder, ready to come up, ready to be aimed at the slightest provocation. Around them, debris—splinters of wood, stone, mud—covers the damp pavement. In the middle distance stand a series of what may have been houses, the remnants of a wall framing a phantom window the only way to determine what they might have been. And beyond that, in the background, a great mountain range, high and blue in the distance, snowcapped and stunning in its beauty, totally unconcerned by it all.

34

Jonas wakes up and cannot move. He wakes up and sees his dead mother at the foot of his bed. He wakes up floating over the world, totally unconnected and able to see everything, everyone in it. He wakes up and thinks he is dead. He wakes up and wishes he were. He wakes up and then goes back to sleep.

He wakes up wishing that he could be back on the mountain, because at least then he knew the score: Either you lived or you died, and it was all just that simple. He wakes up realizing both that something needs to change, and that he doesn't know how to change it.

Then one day he wakes up knowing deeply in his heart that someday soon he is not going to wake up.

35

The groups Rose helps to organize will grow and change and adapt according to their own needs, in their own time. Friendships will be forged. They will gather at someone's house, or in a bar, or at a football game, huddled before and after around a smoking grill in the parking lot, or at a park on a Saturday afternoon, bringing with them their girlfriends and their wives and their children. They will meet up in pairs or in large groups. They will gather at irregular intervals and in various locations. It will start with a phone call, or a message, or a random meeting on some city street, and they will come together, and they will remember.

In one of these groups, standing loosely around a barbecue, they will remember that the barracks was little more than a cinder-block enclosure with a corrugated metal roof. They will remember that, unbelievably in that godforsaken desert, it was raining when they filed back in, the only rain any of them can remember from the whole tour. Their heads hang down, and they are little more than shadows wrapped in ponchos, which are gradually stripped off and left dripping from nails on the wall, or draped over the ends of steel bunk frames. In silence stark as death, they sit on the edges of their bunks, or on the floor, their legs stretched out in front of them and their backs propped against the wall. Or they just stand, jaws drooping and shoulders slouched.

But this is not quite correct, one of them will say, taking a swig from a bottle of beer, poking at the glowing charcoal. This is not quite the way it was. It was not raining, was it? It rained the day Jacobs got killed. Not only that, but at that time, they did not yet know. It was only the day after they went in, remember, and at that time they hadn't known for sure, thought he might still be out there, hunkered beside a rock somewhere. In fact, one lone voice will say, when they filed into the barracks they were concerned, curious, but optimistic. It was raining, sure thing, but they were not yet in mourning, as they tried to piece together the events, tried to determine where it might all have gone wrong.

36

But we weren't done.

I didn't have time to think much about Jezebel because the second company arrived, and then it was time to go in.

I did not know that we were that capable. We bombed the hell out of that place. We had come up the river with great intelligence. We knew who was there, in the village. They told us they were the guys who ambushed us, who killed Jacobs.

We came up the river, and they told us about the village, about the bad guys who were in there. The place was crawling with them, they said. They were all excited about it when they told us. It's a free-fire zone, they said, so stay aggressive. If you see anyone, odds are they're muj. We got 'em, they said. They'll never know what hit 'em, they said. They're there, you know, right where we thought they'd be. We thought they'd be there and there they were. We came up the river, which took us most of the night, and then we got position on them up on this hill. Then there was the standoff all that afternoon, while we waited for reinforcements.

We buried the girl in the moonlight, and then we moved out.

It was all laid out in front of us, the whole thing, just like they told us it would be. I knew what we could do. Well, I thought I knew what we could do. Turns out I had never seen them unleashed like that. They wanted a fight. That river is rough, you know? We figured that would be the hardest part. But we did it. We got position on them, up on that rise, all laid out in front of us.

I did it. I was on the radio, so it was down to me. I got the signal, and I started calling ordnance in, and that place just lit up. Just rained on them. And then we went in, fast. Your heart rate goes up, and we had to go in hard, but it didn't seem real.

Or maybe, when I look back on it now, it seemed so real that everything else seems fake.

A couple of them started shooting back, pretty scattered, but we lit them up fast. And then we get in, and there's just rubble *everywhere. By that time, it's just a big debris field, you know. And every once in a while, someone takes a shot at us, but we clear it out quick.*

And then we were going down this street, and we came around a corner, and there's . . . It was just broken. Everywhere, rocks and stones and rubble. And over there is a body that just looks like another pile of clothes, and a leg sticking up through the rubble here, but this isn't the worst part. Not by a long shot.

Because I look, and there, in the middle of this, there's . . . in this, I don't know, what used to be a house or something, sitting in between all the stones, there is this little child. He's a toddler. He's holding on to this scrap of blanket or something, and he wasn't even crying. That was the worst part. His face was blank, and he just stared up at us, and there was nothing moving anywhere around him, and he looked right at me. And I remember thinking, as I looked at this kid holding on to a blanket in the middle of that rubble: This is my fault. I did this.

And then they must have regrouped or something, because all of a sudden everything opened up all around us. It was like every man, woman, and child in the place suddenly had a weapon, and they were all aimed at us. I didn't fire another shot, though. I kept my weapon up. Okay, once or twice I shot at a wall around somebody, to scare them, or over their heads.

But the whole time I thought to myself: Fuck this.

That's when I saw the kid. He was older, early teens maybe, and for a long time he just stood there in the street. My first thought when I saw him was, He'd better get himself out of here, or he's done.

And then that's exactly what he did. Just like that. Like I thought it and he did it. He ducked back between two houses, heading east, down toward the river.

And then I thought, Maybe I'd better get myself out of here, too.

To my surprise, I followed him.

I just started walking. Made the decision and went down between the same two houses he did. I know it doesn't make sense. None of it makes sense. What if I had followed him down there and a bunch of his friends were there waiting? What if he was sent in there specifically to lure unsuspecting idiots like me back where his brothers could pop them? But that didn't happen.

He was simply trying to get out.

Same as me.

37

The last time he saw his home, he was five thousand feet above it.

Sometimes it comes back to him at a word or a sound. Distantly he hears footfalls and stones clattering. Their muffled voices rise and fall, rise and fall, as he drifts in and out of consciousness, each time their words coming closer and closer before drifting away again in a fog. Something hard pokes him in the ribs.

"Dude's still breathing," someone says.

"Be careful. You never know," says someone else.

He feels a hand on his arm, feels himself being rolled over.

"He's just a kid," says someone. A hand now behind his head, his leg is moved. He is being examined, prodded. The wind whips up the slope, whistling in his ear.

"No way he stitched that up by himself," someone says.

He feels himself lifted from the ground, reaches out with his arm but touches only air. He panics, but it is a distant panic, kept away by the deep haze.

"Whoa, easy there, buddy!" someone says, and then another voice screaming, hard against his head, *"Remain calm. We will help you."*

He tries to clear his vision, and at last resolves the blurry image of two men, one at his head and the other, with his back to him, at his feet. The man at his feet stumbles over something, nearly dropping him onto the rocks, and a distant stab of pain pierces his arm. He hears himself moan.

"Watch it," says a voice. "You're gonna drop him over the edge."

"Easier walk back if I do," says another.

The noise has been there all along, but he becomes aware of it only as it gets louder, through the haze, drowns out the voices, the footfalls, the clattering rocks, the wind. The distant *thump-thump-thump* gets louder and louder until he can feel it, waves of pressure echoing in his head and thudding through his chest, and a violent wind presses down upon every inch of his body.

He feels himself lifted from the world, and then he is a falcon riding high on the thermals, unattached, unhindered, a hundred feet, a thousand feet; he is borne up and away. As the giant bird banks sharply, he is able, for a moment, to bring the earth into focus.

There is the river, rendered tiny and powerless from this odd angle, like a rivulet from an overturned water bucket, and there is the road beside it, and a miniature truck kicking up dust as it careens along in slow motion. He strives to fix his location, struggles to place himself into context, but everything is skewed and unfamiliar.

But when he sees his village, there is no mistaking it. There is the road angling back from the river, and there are the ruins of the caravanserai, where the river road branches apart as it enters the town, and there is the village itself, its streets and houses and fenced-in yards with their orchards. And there is a smoke-blackened house, and there is another, its walls knocked almost casually over, and there is another, still smoldering gently, releasing a single thin tendril of smoke, like a beckoning finger.

And there above it all is Younis, about to pass out again, but conscious for an instant, and aware, and focused, taking it all in, committing the scene to memory, vowing to himself that, if he can recall nothing else, he will always remember this.

38

Monday, November 10 (AP)—The U.S. military has stated that it is investigating a raid conducted last month.

American soldiers apparently believed they were attacking an insurgent hideout in a remote village, and residents of the village claim the Americans killed at least eighteen people. By all accounts, U.S. soldiers arrived before dawn and hit several targets, after an extensive air and artillery barrage.

But beyond that, there appears to be little agreement about what actually happened.

At the first target, the district government offices, they destroyed ammunition, killed four guards, and captured twenty-seven prisoners. But according to some residents, those captured were gunmen loyal to a local politician, plus six people they described as common criminals, pulled out of the local jail. Other residents, however, report that those captured and killed had been inciting violence against international forces for months. While some locals say that the insurgents abandoned the offices weeks ago, others say the building's occupants were heavily involved in insurgent activity.

Another target was a former school building. Armed men were living there, and the U.S. military believes the building had become an insurgent hideout. But once again, locals disagree about who occupied the building. According to some residents and officials, it was actually the headquarters of a local disarmament commission, where officials were collecting weapons from the countryside; others say it was the headquarters of a well-armed insurgent faction.

The morning after the raid, a disarmament commission official says he found vehicles full of bullet holes, gaps blown into the walls, and bodies strewn across three classrooms. Residents say some of the dead men's wrists were bound with plastic handcuffs, evidence that some prisoners were tied up and shot. A U.S. military spokesman disputes this allegation, however, claiming that the prisoners were already dead when soldiers arrived at the location.

At least one source, who spoke on condition of anonymity, reports that the targeted village had been confused with another village some fifty miles away. According to local sources, some families of the dead have already received compensation from the United States—paid in American hundred-dollar bills. It is unclear whether this is true, and, if it is, what criteria were used to distribute this money.

For now, at least, the U.S. military is standing behind its assertion that the government offices and former school building were used by an insurgent operation.

The raid also resulted in the wounding of three U.S. soldiers. The whereabouts of a fourth soldier are still unknown. Several buildings described as private residences were also destroyed; and some inhabitants are still unaccounted for.

Several villagers say the Americans attacked buildings that had become headquarters for two competing political factions. Each faction accuses the other of feeding false information to the U.S. military, tricking the soldiers into destroying its opposition.

Other officials describe the raid not as a conspiracy, but a mistake, suggesting that locals inadvertently gave the American forces flawed intelligence.

Pentagon officials have said thus far that they have received conflicting information about the scope and nature of the operation.

39

I am here by choice. I am ready to accept the consequences of my actions. As I look back, I can see plainly that every choice I have ever made, every action, big or small, was like a single brick in the road leading me here. I will accept responsibility.

I am ready. Tonight I will tell him. He must suspect already. I will tell him, or maybe I will let him read it himself, here, in these pages, where I have laid it out as honestly as I am able. Either way, he should know the truth.

And then everything can either fall apart or hang together, or go whichever way it will.

40

"Hello," he says to the small circle of chairs. "My name is Jonas."

"Hello, Jonas," comes the reply, like a chant. And then a single voice, gentle in the quiet room, says, "And, Jonas, how long has it been since you last had a drink?"

But there is no reply.

The silence stretches on, longer than it seems it should. It grows to encompass the room. Some of those present realize what's going on before others, and they look up. One by one, those gathered in the circle, those whose heads had been bowed as though in thought or prayer, those who had been staring at the walls or the floor, the one or two who held their eyes gently closed, lift their heads to look at the figure sitting in the chair next to the door, his head held in his hands, his body shaking with sobs.

ATONEMENT

Occasionally Jonas hears the voice of his savior.

It comes to him when he is unable to turn his thoughts to anything else. The voice he hears is gentle and deep. When he remembers it, he tries to get it right, tries to match the words exactly, but has the familiar feeling that he is adding and subtracting, substituting what should have been said for what he fails to remember accurately.

What should have been said. What he fails to remember.

He is haunted by both.

You probably wonder why I want you to read this, why I am telling you all this.

I know who you are. We came to your village, all laid out in the moonlight. We were up on the rise, and then we were like a wave, relentless, effective, crashing down the hill.

I had enough. We snapped. Something snapped. I snapped. And then I followed you here.

I know who you are. I saw you leave. I followed you. I tracked you down the river, watched you turn toward the hills at the balancing rock, chased you up and over the stony slope, looked on as you lost your path and then found it again, lost it and then found it once more.

I watched you. I had to talk to you. I had to explain. I had to make you understand. I had to ask your forgiveness.

And here I lie, prostrate in the dust before you.

Waiting.

3

Jonas wakes in sheets soaked with sweat. He is haunted. He gets out of bed, grabs a T-shirt. He has seen two versions of the future. He gathers together everything he has saved from the packet, every letter, every photocopied photograph, every newspaper clipping, even the envelope itself, labeled in Rose's flowing script in blue ink, labeled "Christopher."

He sees two versions of his future. Then he sees three. Then he sees a thousand, each a slightly distorted reflection of the others, all of them shining back at him like pieces of a shattered mirror.

He goes out into the night. The cold air smells like snow, and his arms prickle in the wind. Picking his path along the cracked cement sidewalk, he makes his way to the park beside the river, next to the railroad bridge on Fourteenth Street.

He has seen himself grown and married, the father of a young child. As he walks to the river, he avoids the cracks in the cement, as though stepping on one of them will open a chasm through which he will fall and be lost. He has seen himself as a criminal, as a murderer, as someone entirely able to rationalize what he has become. He can hear the river before he gets to it, the roar of the rapids out in the middle, seemingly unconnected to the calm, shallow water near the shore. But he knows that a stick or a leaf, floating in the shallows, can be suddenly caught up and taken out and away, into the roaring tempest.

But this is inaccurate. The river is quiet, its flowing volumes of water pouring silent and deep. The yellowed street lamps light his way. To get to the park, he must descend a steep embankment, past a fenced-in cemetery, its standing tombstones pointing toward God. As he struggles near the top of the slope, he trips on a rock, twisting his ankle, and nearly falls over the side, into the river below.

The last time he saw his home, he was five thousand feet above it. He cannot quiet his mind. He has read the Bible he has been given. He has read that God is loving and kind, and then that He is jealous. He has read somewhere else that Jesus died for his sins. He has read that the meek shall inherit the earth, and he does not want any part of it.

The shrill air brings his life to the top of his skin.

He stands with difficulty, takes an agonizing step, his ankle throbbing each time his foot hits the cold ground. He struggles with categories. He can neither place himself into context, nor can he be placed. The usual labels fail. He is a victim. He is a perpetrator. He is a terrorist. He is a refugee. He feels himself placed neatly into boxes. He fights against labels. He is omniscient. He is a criminal.

He has gathered everything together, everything he has, all the physical proof that tells him who he is, who Christopher was, and he takes it all down to the park, next to the bridge, which spans the river pouring dark and wide below. He is a man. He is a boy. He is human. He is an alien.

He wants to burn it, burn everything associated with it, burn his past and send it skyward in a burst of smoke and sparks. He is an arsonist. He is a fireman. He is an archivist. He is a vandal. He has arrived at the park, limping on his twisted ankle, and has placed the sheaf of papers on the ground next to a large boulder before he realizes that he has forgotten to bring any matches.

He is incompetent.

He comes up with another plan. He climbs back up the steep embankment, up to the base of the bridge, climbs the brief stone staircase and grabs hold of the bridge's rusting, cast-iron service ladder. He lives in the buckle of the rust belt. He climbs the ladder and walks out onto a narrow metal catwalk suspended underneath the bridge. He is the product of generations spent in wind and cold. He belongs, secure in his mobile community. He is an outsider. He wonders who has a greater claim to the truth, himself or those who would label him. His darkness is palpable. He skews the demographic.

The rusting catwalk sways under his steps, and he feels each footfall echo through the metal. Maybe he is just like anyone of a certain age. Or maybe he is not. Maybe he is such the product of loss that his soul reeks of it.

He walks on the catwalk out into the middle of the bridge, high over the water. The night is quiet, and he hears the traffic onshore, an airplane passing high overhead, on its way to somewhere else.

He feels the train before he sees it. The rails above him begin to sing with a high-pitched, metallic sound, like the highest note of a chorus of violins, and then he hears what sounds like a hundred flags cracking in the wind, and an engine noise like a broken scooter, and underneath that is a low whistle, like his father calling to the sheep, the whole cacophony getting louder and louder and stretching on until forever. The catwalk jumps and shakes, and the single light on the front of the train's engine lights up the tracks like daytime, so that Jonas can see nothing in the harsh glare. He grips the railing, grips also the packet of papers that tells him who he is. The train passes only feet over his head, shaking the catwalk until his shoes bounce from its surface. He begins to scream, not out of pain or fear or panic, but words, fully formed, screams, enumerates for the world all that has been taken from him, all that he has lost, but finds the words inaudible underneath the roaring train.

And then it is almost instantaneously silent. Subtle noises

return in the wake, the river's gurgle, the traffic on the shore, the distant echo of a tugboat's horn.

Almost as an afterthought, he tosses the sheaf of papers off of the bridge.

As they fly through the air, the pages reflect faintly the meager light from headlights and street lamps onshore. He watches them fly. Many of the pages stick more or less together, forming a relatively solid, plummeting mass, leading the way through the chill air for other individual sheets of paper, which expand, separate from themselves, become a multitude of individual pages, fluttering down, all of them finding their way, eventually, into the pitch-black. They settle silently onto the river's surface, where they remain dimly visible for a time, white sparks floating in the night, until they gradually log with water, and disappear.

4

Someone will buy a round, and someone else will speak up. Remember the river, they will say. Remember how rough it was, the rapids frothy as though a giant blender churned on the riverbed deep below us. Which boat were you in? someone will ask. Oh, that's right, someone else will say, suddenly remembering something he swore at the time he would never forget. And then there was Chris, remember, Henderson in the bow, pointing us through the rapids.

And do you remember that moon, someone will say, that

thin crescent moon slung low in the sky? I have never since seen a moon quite like that one, the way the tiny little sliver of it seemed to light up the whole valley, the whole world, the whole future in front of us, dusted with light.

5

The next morning, Jonas has a plan. He decides that he wants to talk. There is something he knows he must do. His life now revolves around it.

He is suddenly wide-awake, and looks out the window to see that winter has descended like a thick, white duvet. He is out of bed, fighting against the cold of his room. He turns the shower on, hot enough to make him wince, swaying his body under the stream. He is nervous, excited, feels the tension bunch in his stomach and run down his arms to his fingers. He feels himself on the verge of flight.

Outside, he has to concentrate to keep from slipping on the packed snow as his footsteps take him, almost of their own will, to Paul's office.

"All right," says Paul. "Why now?"

"Because there is something I have to do, and it starts with this."

Jonas watches his distorted reflection in Paul's silver statue. He wants to get it out, he says. He has a plan.

But he senses that Paul's energy has subtly changed. He feels it in the room when he arrives. It's nothing overt, at first.

Paul seems a little distracted, that's all. He seems to be marginally less interested in hearing what Jonas has to say, and Jonas assumes that it is because he is thinking about something else.

Nevertheless, Jonas carries on, tells him about the night he left his village, tells him about fleeing into the mountains, about finding the cave, about losing consciousness in the cold and wind, about meeting Christopher there, about how Christopher stitched him up, fed him, built him a fire.

But still he feels that something has changed. Paul wants to hear, he says, wants to know what happened, and still thinks Jonas needs to tell it.

"Then what's the problem?" asks Jonas.

"I'm concerned," says Paul. "I'm concerned about what happened. I'm worried it might be something I have to report. But I'm not sure. I have no experience with this. I have no idea what the law says about this."

Jonas has never seen Paul unable to find his words, or act awkward or ill at ease, and he finds the sight of it troubling.

"Look," says Paul, "let me make a phone call, okay? It shouldn't take too long. I just want to be sure I'm not going to get you into trouble."

And so Jonas is left alone in Paul's office, left alone to contemplate the enigmatic statue on the desk, left to watch his distorted reflection play across its surface.

Paul comes back into the office after a few minutes, but it is Jonas who speaks.

"I've been thinking," says Jonas. "I trust you. This has to come out. You have convinced me of that. This is going to consume me. I don't need a shrink to tell me that." He glances again at the statue on Paul's desk, and thinks to himself that this will probably be the last time he sees it.

"Yes," says Paul, "but as I told you, I am obligated. It's a legal thing. It's not my choice. It may seem arbitrary, I know."

"But what could happen?"

"In reality, I don't know, for sure. Maybe nothing. Maybe they would just come and talk to you. Maybe they would issue a warrant for your arrest. It's hard to tell. They've been taking this stuff pretty seriously lately."

"But it is your choice *when* you tell them, right?"

"Sorry?"

"You don't have to report it today, right?"

"I don't think there is a time . . . I don't know."

"You could give me a few days. You could fill out the form, file the report or make the phone call, or do whatever it is that you have to do, and if anyone ever asks, you could tell them that you did it as soon as you were able. You could do that, right?"

Paul tugs absently at the hair in his goatee, and lets out a long sigh.

"I could," he says at last. "Look, nobody is forcing you."

"I know," says Jonas. "That's why I'm going to do it."

"This makes no sense."

"Don't you see? It's the same thing. You'll be helping me. Forcing me to go. Helping me to do something difficult. Just like Christopher helped me."

"Christopher helped you. You mean when he saved you?"

"No, at the end. When he helped me do it. He knew. He

helped me do it. He knew what would happen, what had to happen. He set it up to happen. He knew."

"He knew what?"

"He knew who I was. He tracked me up there. He set it up to happen."

"Set up what, Jonas?"

"He had to know what I would do. He had to. He just had to."

6

Younis has been lying with his eyes open for hours, lying at the edge of the cave, the dying fire flickering shadows against the rock wall. He has been listening, waiting for Christopher's breath to calm, regularize into the pattern of sleep. He knows now what will happen, what has to happen. He will be purposeful about it. Deliberate. It will be fast. He will grant him that. Speed will be the only good in it.

He knows where the knife will be, honed and hard and cold, its hilt protruding from the rocky soil. He has measured, in his mind, the distance. He is convinced that even Christopher understands what must happen. For has he not told him what to do? Has he not placed the knife in the ground each night, each night slightly farther away from himself and slightly closer to Younis? Does he merely imagine it?

He listens for the breath, the gentle rhythm, the peace. He vows that he will not even wake him. Silently he makes this promise to both of them. He will be swift, precise. The decision has already been made. There will be no pain, no struggle. Just peace. His own desires are no longer a consideration. What will happen is what must happen, what is fated to happen. What has been decided.

Afterward, he will roll his body gently off the cliff. He will scatter some earth after him. He will say a few words, low and heartfelt, about loss, about God, about how sorry he is that it had to be this way.

Then he will sit down on a rock and read the book, cover to cover. He will linger over some passages, and skim through others. He will place the book gently under a rock at the back of the cave, confident that he is the only one in the world who knows where it is.

But for now, he is being pulled along, set in motion, his own will no longer figuring into it. He listens again for the breath, calculates his position.

And then—does he imagine it?—Christopher opens his eyes.

For a moment they see each other, a blink, and Younis hesitates. Within a moment they meet. Younis realizes what he is about, feels the weight of a moment that will stretch, in his mind, into an eternity.

And then his eyes are closed.

And then he is motion.

He pops into the air like a gazelle, a blur, silent, focused, springing to his feet and across the rocky precipice in a single action, and the knife is exactly where he knew it would be, and it is in his hand, unsheathed from the earth.

He sees himself as though from the outside, detached, as though it is someone else doing it. And from this place, this disembodied vantage, he sees himself, now a flash, darting across the open space, now merging with the figure prone on the ground, now springing up to stand over him, taut and ready.

And he is surprised by how easy it is, how quiet, how neatly the knife's sharp edge slits his sleeping throat, how simple, like a stone plopping into water.

BENEDICTION

I

One year the group rents out the Carlisle Auditorium in Pittsburgh. The next, they are booked into the Bethel Park Recreation Center. The following year they are given an anonymous donation, which allows them to rent out a portion of the convention center. The group calling itself Military Families for Truth grows, changes, adapts. Other groups take root, sprout up in other parts of the country. The fertile soil of the Southeast, Florida, Georgia, the Carolinas, others in the rocks and scrub of Arizona, Utah, still others under the Northwest rain.

Rose leads a delegation to Capitol Hill, to talk with the representatives in Congress. A member from Michigan introduces himself. He has heard of Rose, and asks her to speak with his colleagues. Loss has come to his state, he tells her, and who is Rose if not loss's spokesperson?

She develops bureaucratic skill. She familiarizes herself with grant applications and donor forums and aid requests. She learns how to advocate for or against legislation, how to submit requests under the Freedom of Information Act, learns who makes the decisions at particular government agencies, and how to most effectively apply pressure to them.

The groups grow, change, merge. Local groups combine into regional groups, which then become national collectives. An umbrella organization is formed, called the Associated Families of Veterans, and Rose is elected its first president.

And yet, despite her tireless efforts, the meticulous attention to detail, it is so often the role of chance or luck that brings her any form of comfort, any sense of closure. An e-mail message, which she now sends and receives proficiently, arrives one day as though from a cloud, or a chance encounter at a meeting or conference, someone who seeks her out, happens across her path.

So it is that Rose finds herself walking across the cavernous expanse of yet another convention center, this one in Denver or Chicago or Albuquerque, her great plume of red hair now streaked liberally with white, walking quickly, purposefully, because she is late to be somewhere else and the place is so big that it takes forever to get anywhere. She sees him from the corner of her eye, peripherally, before she hears his voice.

"Excuse me," he says, and she does not want to be rude, does not want to appear uninterested, but she is late and the appointment is important and . . .

"Excuse me," says the man again, and now Rose sees no way out. She turns to look at him, make contact with him.

"Are you Rose Henderson?" he says as he approaches.

Rose tilts her head back to look up at him. He is balding, his hair cut short in an attempt to cover the fact. He looks to be approaching middle age. He has powerfully built shoulders and arms, but is developing a paunch around his middle.

"I am," says Rose, concentrating on him, now that she has been stopped, giving him her full attention.

"I thought so," says the man. "I've seen your picture. You don't know me, but I served with Christopher."

"Oh," says Rose. "I see. Well, let's . . . let's step over here."

2

Jonas walks down the fluorescent corridor. Travelers rush past him pulling wheeled suitcases or hunched under weighty backpacks. The small sack he carries over his shoulder has floated through security with ease, and his stuffed duffel lies, perhaps already, in the hold of the plane. Despite this, he is convinced that the policemen have been looking at him, regarding him closely. He does not know what Paul has said, whom he has contacted, or even whether, in fact, he has said anything, but he is convinced that it is only a matter of time. A young woman hurries ahead of him, gripping her child's hand.

"Come on," says the woman to the unconcerned boy. "They're already boarding."

He steps onto the swift conveyor, adjusting his balance as the belt takes over. He is being pulled along now, set in motion, no longer entirely under his own power.

He finds the bathroom at the far end of the corridor, conveniently located just across from the gate. Inside, past the row of sinks, the faucets of which are hooked to motion sensors and seem to flow randomly, as though ghosts are washing their hands, he spots the trash can, stainless steel and set into the wall. He pauses, has a thought. He waits for everyone to leave, for the bathroom to empty, a lull, and then he walks over to the trash can. He reaches into it, rummages around.

There is nothing, no nylon straps, no vest, just a trash bag half-filled with damp paper towels. A man walks in and looks at him askance, looks at him with his arm stuck shoulder-deep into the rubbish bin, and he feels foolish. It all comes down to this, he thinks. A choice. The difference between two realities, each of them real, balanced on a knife edge in time.

A voice, commanding and feminine, announces his flight over the public address system, echoing from the tiled walls. The bathroom has filled with people, and he is momentarily confused, unable to find the exit. When at last he does, he joins the throng of travelers, of fathers and mothers and aunts and brothers struggling under the weight of luggage and worry, or buoyed by excitement and anticipation, or driven by determined focus.

When he gets to the gate, he finds that his flight has been delayed. There is some sort of last-minute equipment problem. The irritated crowd, which had just been preparing to board the plane, lets out a collective breath. With nothing else to do, he finds a seat in the waiting area and watches as the passengers huddle around the gate, waiting in the limbo of the airline terminal for time to restart.

He decides he will conduct an experiment. A clean-cut young Indian man wearing a starched dress shirt, the sleeves rolled up to the elbows, gestures urgently as he converses with a disengaged airline representative behind the counter. Jonas was told about it, this experiment, something a monk he once met did whenever he was in public. An overweight couple arrives pushing an overweight toddler in a fragile-looking stroller. Jonas calms his breath, concentrating on nothing more than inhaling and exhaling. He will look each person he encounters in the eyes. To each of them, to every person who meets his gaze, he will wish peace. A tall, thin, elderly gentleman wearing a cowboy hat leans over toward a gray-haired woman who barely comes to his chest, their heads nearly touching, their arms entwined, as they converse in hushed tones. He watches them all as they mill about, or rush to the snack bar to get something to drink, or stare at their laptop screens.

He is unhurried, the swirl of activity surrounding him but not touching him. A dark-skinned gentleman wearing a tan fedora arrives late, carrying a leather briefcase, and approaches the counter, confident, as though it is him for whom everyone has assembled. Jonas regards them inclusively, looking at each as they stand or pass by, male, female, young, old, infirm, healthy, offering to each his attention. Jonas spots a girl about his age, tall, with dark hair and graceful legs, and he stops for a moment, because he thinks that she looks striking and familiar.

Many of them don't see him, are too busy or preoccupied. Some of them see that he is looking at them and look away, at the floor, or at something that has become suddenly interesting. Some of them look up at him and smile.

Mostly, it is the elderly and the children who notice.

3

Through the brightly lit corridors they move, and the cavernous meeting halls, and the convention centers, the high school gymnasiums, the temples, synagogues, and churches. They bustle about or sit and talk among themselves, the wives and children and parents and classmates and friends and girlfriends and comrades. They ask questions, and they provide answers. They mill about, or they rush frenetically. They talk about both the future and the past, starting their conversations with, "What we will do . . ." and "I remember when . . ."

At one of these places, at one of these times, two of them stand temporarily still, apart from the movement and energy around them, and they talk, allowing it all to pass them by, like a river roaring over the rocks.

He is telling Rose about her son, about the strength he drew from him, about how much he meant, about the comfort of his presence, about the last time he was seen alive.

"I remember when," he is saying. "I remember when we were on that rise above the village, before we went in. I looked up, and he was on the hill right there above me. I had just transferred in. It was my first time in combat. The other guys, they were itching for a fight. There was a lot of talk. Talk about payback, revenge. They had lost some guys before I got there. I tried to sympathize, talk a good game, but really I was just scared out of my wits.

"And there he was up above me on the rise, looking out at the valley, at that village in front of us in the moonlight. He was quiet, calm. I think he was always like that. He turned around to look at me. They were all getting themselves angry, worked up. But not him. He didn't think that way. My face must have been so white it shone like that moon. He must have noticed, because he looked down at me with the calm look he had, the one that told you everything was going to be okay, and he patted me on the helmet, smiled a little, like he was resigned to something. It was just one of those moments, one of those things that pass by at the time and you barely even notice it, but then you remember it for the rest of your life.

"That's what I want to tell you. That's why I came here. I remember when I looked at him up on that hill, and the moon was low in the sky behind him, and he reached down and patted me on the helmet, and he nodded at me. And then the radio squawked through our earpieces, and the order came down, and just that fast he was up and over the rise.

"Just that fast. A silhouette, and then he was gone."

RECESSIONAL

I

He changes his name on the airplane. Somewhere over a distant sea, he resumes his old identity. He prints his name—Y-O-U-N-I-S—in the spaces demarcated on the landing card he has been given. In his mind, the landing card increases in significance, becomes something more, a part of the trail of evidence. All this paper, he thinks. All these little ways of telling him who he is.

He goes back. This is the point. As he has done obsessively the entire trip, he shoves his hand into his pants pocket to make sure he still has the scrap of paper, now creased and torn, with Rose's address printed neatly on one side.

And then he imagines himself descending from the bright airplane and into a dry, desert wind that envelops him like a wave. The peaks of the far southern mountains are jagged saw teeth in the distance. Everything is returned to the way it was.

Someone will be there to greet him, a cousin, because his father was unable to make the trip, suddenly called away on some pressing business. But someone will be sent, someone who is happy to see him, and they will drive in a battered white truck up into the hills. They will drive beside the river, the raging torrent in the middle seemingly unconnected to the calm shallows at the edge, but he will know that this is an illusion, that in fact the shallows and the torrent are one.

Despite its inner turmoil, even the river will be happy to see him there, returned.

He will find everything the same. He will see things that are familiar, comforting. The colors, for example, will feel familiar, the red ochre rocks of the foothills, the bleached walls of the houses lining the road. He will be reminded of things he forgot he ever knew. The smells in particular will trigger lucid memories. He will recognize faces, see old friends, be returned to his former self, play in the courtyard with his sister, gratefully receive his mother's tea. He will traverse the upturned sod, wander the low pastures with the flock and the dogs. All that which maintains a hold upon him will lose its grip.

Somewhere over a distant sea he realizes that this is all a fantasy. He will not be greeted by his family. He will recognize little. Perhaps nothing will feel familiar. He will step once again into the unknown.

And so, in the end, he does not change his name. The plane has begun its descent, and the attendants wander the aisles. A bell dings. He feels the sinking sensation in his stomach. He makes a decision. He knows it will cause trouble, but he does it anyway. He glances again at the landing card, at the name printed in black ink, printed in his own handwriting.

And then he tears it up.

2

The parcel arrives unexpectedly in the spring.

It's the first truly warm day of the year, the young leaves and buds only just emerging from the long winter. Rose works in her backyard, spading a hole in the ground large enough to accommodate the sapling that leans on burlap-wrapped roots against the stone wall. Rose thinks that perhaps she is being overly optimistic, planting an oak at her age. She pulls off her gloves and smoothes her graying hair away from her face. Her breath is quickened by her labor, and the earth under her spade looks wounded. She looks around at the new spring leaves' fresh pastels. She hears the mail truck rattle to a halt out front. Reluctant to stop working, she hesitates before she leans the spade against the wall next to the waiting tree, and goes to get the mail.

The parcel is wrapped in brown paper and plastered with green-and-blue stamps and exotic writing. It feels dense and heavy in her hands, the thick paper wrapper crisp and new. Curious, she takes the package inside, sits down at the kitchen table, and begins to remove the wrapping.

She recognizes it instantly.

The book's leather cover is heavily worn at the edges, scuffed and scratched, creased at the spine, and a thin leather tie holds it closed, tied in a precise knot.

It looks, she thinks, like it has been through a war.

Her hand trembles a little as she gently tugs at the knot and opens the front cover. There, beside the compass rose inscribed on the frontispiece, is a brief dedication written in her own flowing script:

> *For Chris,*
> *On your eighteenth birthday.*
> *Because your words are important.*
>
> *Love,*
> *Mom*

Rose sits at the kitchen table, her head in her hand, the book open before her. The thin spring sunlight filters in through the window. In the backyard, a young tree leans against an old stone wall, ready to heal the wounded earth. The season is young, the fragile new foliage painting the world pastel. Rose turns the page, begins to read, and is free.

Acknowledgments

The creation of this book has removed any notion I might have held of its being a solo endeavor. I am grateful to so many.

I owe tremendous debts of gratitude to both the world's greatest agent, Henry Dunow, for recognizing what this story could be in its better form, for his unfailing advocacy, and for his willingness to take a chance, and to the world's greatest editor, Sarah Hochman, for her confidence, enthusiasm, and nearly perfect editorial guidance. Tremendous thanks go as well to everyone else at Blue Rider Press and Penguin who have made this book what it is: David Rosenthal, Aileen Boyle, Kate Guadagnino, and Jaya Miceli. Never has an author felt in better hands.

Before there was a book, there was manuscript, and an author thereof, both of which benefited tremendously from merely being in the presence of Bret Anthony Johnston, Amy Hempel, Nick Montemorano, Rachel Pastan, and Brian Morton.

Like many teachers, Judith Vollmer probably had no idea what kind of impact she was making at the time she was making it, but I count her among the reasons I never stopped writing. I am particularly grateful for another of those reasons, my family: Paul Dau, Susan Reed, Michelle Dupuis, and Matthew Dau, for whom the simple fact that I wanted to do something was always reason enough to support it unconditionally, and to my father-in-law, Dr. Zackariya-Marikar, who routinely seems to make anything possible. Special thanks go as well to Tod Goldberg, for offering solid advice, both practical and metaphysical; to my talented and generous Bennington classmates, for their encouragement, enthusiasm, support, and for repeatedly reminding me what can be done with words; and, of course, to Jon Lyons.

And I am always grateful to my daughter, Seraphina, for giving me everything in the world to smile about, and for forgiving Papa the hours spent away, and to my wife, Claudia, who asked me, right after we met, what I wanted to do with my life. I told her that I had wanted to write since I was eight years old, and she said simply, "Then do it." She has not wavered once.